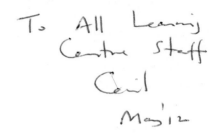

To All Learning
Centre Staff
Cecil
May'12

Cecil Browne was born in St Vincent and the Grenadines, SVG, in 1957. He attended Byera Anglican School and the Boys Grammar School. In 1970 he left for England to join his parents.

He has been a lecturer for twenty-seven years, ten as Head of Maths in a College of Further Education. His first book, *The Moon Is Following Me*, was published in 2010.

D1369062

feather your tingaling

cecil browne

Matador
9 Priory Business Park,
Wistow Road
Kibworth Beauchamp
Leicester LE8 0RX, UK
Tel: (+44) 116 279 2299
Fax: (+44) 116 279 2277
Email: books@troubador.co.uk
Web: www.troubador.co.uk/matador

ISBN 9781780880877

British Library Cataloguing in Publication Data.
A catalogue record for this book is available from the British Library.

Typeset in 11.5pt Sabon MT by Troubador Publishing Ltd, Leicester, UK

Matador is an imprint of Troubador Publishing Ltd

Printed and bound ind bound in the UK by TJ International, Padstow, Cornwall

Acknowledgement

Once again I thank my wife, Denise, and daughters, Ama and Sable, for their support and patience. To F Herbert, and my sister, Jean, who read the manuscript and made many suggestions, thanks for your critical advice.

Finally, to my family and friends-too many to mention-who helped in the promotion of TMIFM, hope you enjoy this one even more.

contents

Foreword

This collection is a logical successor to *The Moon Is Following Me*. The stories continue the theme, but they also move into new territory.

In *The Moon Is Following Me* I suggested that the village is the centre of Caribbean life. Wherever we go, whenever we meet, the first question is invariably, 'Where are you from?' Characters like Archie from Take For Two were recognisable to readers, hence the success of the collection. *Feather Your Tingaling* introduces new characters, and moves in another direction.

Older readers will remember moonlit nights, perfect for 'ring play', during which an entire village enacted stories for its own entertainment. 'Girl, go feather your tingaling,' we sang as children, not knowing the meaning, but too enraptured to ask, or taking the song as a little piece of nonsense to enliven a beautiful night. 'Brown-skin girl, stay home and mind baby!' we advised, at the top of our voices, repeating the chorus of a song whose origin was hazy even to our parents. In this book I've imagined the source of these two songs, and invented characters on whom the songs might have been based.

Then there's Basil Lincoln. Terrifying but ordinary sounding, who or what was he? Again, I've attempted to bring him alive to readers. Those who don't know him will discover, hopefully, a rich addition to Caribbean folklore and literature.

Like Spanish Ladies from *The Moon Is Following Me*, The Hole, the penultimate story in this book, has elements of truth, the story, Late, also. But both are not based on any individual. Business is Business is loosely based on more austere times in the early seventies. The events were funny then and even now friends remember them affectionately.

Two of the stories, The Circuit and PQR, are set in England, but the Caribbean link is still there. I think you will enjoy them.

Once again I have taken liberties with the geography of SVG.

brown-skin girl

She was the youngest of four sisters, Judith boasted, the Monday evening we met at the bar by Kingstown harbour, they were from Greiggs on the windward side of the island. From her bedroom window you could see the Atlantic, she whispered, in the husky voice I sensed she was putting on for my benefit, the winds lashed their house during the rainy season, but she loved nothing better than a good storm with thunder and lightning!

Dressed in a plain white shirt and loose wine-coloured trousers, exaggerating her courage, I watched her thin arms rise and fall as she told me this, and chuckled softly, wondering what she knew about storms.

I liked Judith immediately. Dark-brown, set well back in the narrow face, her eyes had the sparkling look I liked in women. Bright and alluring, they invited even as they begged to be kind and gentle with her. Her thick black hair, gathered and pinned at the back of her head, exposing the high forehead, her full but soft black cheeks glowing invitingly, I was hooked. Attractive, and knowing it, she played on her looks. She had the verve of a woman accustomed to compliments and knowing glances.

I liked her hair, the slight upturn of her nose, and the fullness of her lips, but her figure was even more impressive. She had 'shape'. She was one of those women, tantalising, whose body easily assumed the contours of their dress, not filling it, but allowing the imagination full play. In shorts, trousers or dressed for dinner, she moved with an unforced elegance that made me glad I was a man. Her motion was easy and fluid, and did she flaunt it!

Even on that first night it was noticeable. Thrice she grabbed her handbag, asked to be excused, and strolled outside 'for some night air'. Each time the entire bar was treated to a performance. I didn't like it. She wasn't exactly my woman then, but her manner, which she later denied, made me uneasy. We had spent two hours eating, drinking and talking, I had answered every request for rum and black. Tucked away in a cosy corner of the noisy bar, in the half-darkness for most of the time, she hoped to see me again, she said. And, provided I wasn't married, she would await my return to SVG. So, even then I was beginning to think of us together. Why the style, then, I wondered, why invite other eyes?

On her last trip outside I began to see things from her point of view. The five minutes she spent clearing her lungs had given me time to think. I was a sailor after all, freshly docked, and I had done what we did on every Caribbean island: race to the nearest bar, find a woman and spend some dollars!

In luscious St Lucia, in fritter-flat Antigua, in bewitching

Martinique where our French patois was truly stretched, we scrambled for the first bar to the left of the dock like nomads to an oasis. To drink every bar dry was our mission. Where we failed, we put that right the night the ship was due to sail. So, the more I thought about it, as Judith escaped the fusion of smoke, liquor and stale perfume of *Joey's* bar, the more I grew to understand how she felt. But, I was to discover, drawing attention to herself was the least of Judith's problems.

I must meet her family, she suggested as she kissed me goodbye that warm Monday night, I would like them, and they would be delighted to meet me. Comfortable, not rich, not poor, theirs was a happy home, she boasted. Her father was brown and her mother black. Like the rest of the village, they were all 'mixed-up'.

It was after eleven by then, Kingstown as quiet as a country village, hardly a vehicle on the street, the ancient cobblestones glistening in the moonlight. At the end of a long hot day the harbour was resting, the waves sliding silently to the shore. From the bar, at regular intervals, came raucous laughter and the screams of couples setting things up for midnight. 'Mixed-up people,' she repeated, inhaling the night air, 'from Lauders to Greiggs, what a confusion!' I didn't fully appreciate the meaning of her remark at the time, for I thought Caribbean people had long since accepted that the entire region was an eclectic mix. Judith seemed to be one of the few who had an issue with this.

'Neil,' she said, as I took a stool next to hers outside the bar, 'thanks for a wonderful evening.'

'I'm glad you enjoy it,' I replied, taking her left hand to show her how much I had appreciated her company.

'You make me feel special. I'm glad I came here tonight.'

'You *are* special,' I said, for it was rare to find a woman who didn't spend the evening talking about herself, but who was genuinely interested in life at sea. 'You don't know that?'

'You can't know some things unless someone tell you.'

'Well, *I'm* telling you.'

'Thanks,' she gave me a peck on the lips. 'You sailor boys full of sweet sea-talk: must be all that time you spend gazing at the stars.'

'You know a lot of sailors?' I asked.

'No: but I know men.'

'How you mean?'

'Men so predictable.'

'You think so?'

'I *know* so.'

'Really?'

'You don't have to pretend with me, Neil. Men full of talk, they treat you nice, they buy you whatever you want: but ask them to take the next step and they vanish like a rounce at three in the morning.'

'You must choose the wrong ones,' I suggested.

'Every man is the wrong man.'

'That's a bit strong.'

'But is true: you all over me tonight, but if you get what you after, Judith Neverson going to disappear from your mind until you in the middle of the ocean, or on a calm night when things quiet at sea.'

'So why you don't tell me to scarper? Why not say, "Thanks for a good time" and go home to your man or your family?'

'Because I'm stupid, I suppose. And because I don't have a man.'

'You don't have a man?' I was both surprised and glad.

'No.'

'What happen to the men on this island, they blight or something?'

'I don't have a man because I don't *want* a man.'

'And why is that?'

'The moment you wish to take a relationship to a higher level is gone man gone: their bank balance erode, they remember they have wife, their baby catch malaria: I could write a book about the men on this blessed island.'

'A *big* book?'

'No, but big enough: if I include all I know, and add what my friends tell me, then you will have reading for a long week on the ship!'

'You sound bitter.'

'Bitter? Nah. Not bitter: just realistic. After a while you come to accept that every man wrong for you.'

'Or you're the wrong woman for them!'

'Could be: You're either too short or too thin, too clever or too stupid. I'm sure I'm too black for some of them.'

'Too *black*? What kind of nonsense is that, Judith?' I was stunned by this statement.

'Some men don't like their women too dark!'

'They tell you that?'

'Not directly, but I could tell: just as well I'm light-skinned: they can't break style on me.

'You're not light-skinned, you're black.'

'No I'm not.'

'You *are*, Judith,' I didn't hold back, 'you, me, Cup-a-Joe, Hilton, Ann-Marie, who hook up with Festus, and her sister Marie-Ann who drunk in the corner, everyone in the bar black: if you can't see that I feel sorry for you.'

'I don't want your sympathy,' she protested. 'I'm lighter than all of them, they not in the same class as me. You and me about the same colour.'

'And I'm black, so that make you black too.'

'Say what you like, Neil, I'm not truly black, I'm brown-skin. My hair long and straight, my father passed down his features to me.' She patted her hair at the sides. 'You think any of the other women in the bar could match my hair?'

'The women in there happy the way they are from what I could see,' I said, thinking how easy it was to undo a beautiful evening.

'That is what you think,' she insisted. 'You're a man, how would you know they happy, you ask them?'

Naturally, I was reluctant to meet her family after this exchange. I didn't quite know what to make of her. It could have been the drink, I told myself, she was probably trying to impress me or to warn me off. But even without those concerns I wouldn't have gone.

The minute a woman introduces you to her mother and her warm hand remains shy and limp in yours, you make plans to flee. The instant her father reticently extends his right hand then gives you that stern look, his head cocked to the left, that slight sneer on his lips, you know you're cutting your own throat. So I told her, 'Not yet, Judith, perhaps the next time. When I come back to SVG, if you haven't found yourself a man, who knows, eh?'

The ship was in for repairs so we had two extra days ashore. We got to know each other, played, talked, swapped our favourite stories. But I was never going to get close to her and, because I was a sailor, I seldom allowed a woman to develop strong feelings for me. A girl in every port? Not quite, I wasn't that kind of guy.

Thirty-seven, short and stocky, round-shouldered, I wasn't a ladies' man. With a dominant nose, large teeth, tight wiry hair, and a forehead that wrinkled when I got excited or cross, I wasn't going to prosper by my looks. Women liked to attach themselves to a sailor, and I had money, it was no use fooling myself. I was generous and I relished their company: from the outset we knew where we stood.

In Barbados I was welcome at *Gussy's*, in Trinidad and Tobago, I didn't have to work too hard. My lack of French and average looks didn't stop me having a beautiful escort, Bernadine Sebastienne, a convent schoolmistress with finely-plaited hair, whenever we sailed north and docked in Guadeloupe. But plain or beautiful, young or old, single or married, the women all knew the score: an evening with Neil Pope meant all the drink they wanted, a bit of dancing, and the best food going. None was obliged to listen to my sailor's tales, or to tell me their life story: when the clock struck twelve, they could return to their homes if they wished.

It wasn't fair on a woman, I often had to remind myself on the verge on intimacy - if it came to that - take it easy Neil boy, do what you have to do, but no more: you never know if and when you would be passing this way again. Do what was necessary, but tell them the truth. Don't make promises you don't intend to keep. Yet, for three days, laughing, hugging and kissing, me and Judith were inseparable. But, deep down, I felt she had latched onto me, short and ordinary, too quickly, and being away at sea for months on end, how could I trust a 'brown-skin girl' with a pretty walk who claimed not to have a man, and who felt superior to other women because of our messy Caribbean history?

I didn't like women for their complexion. They had to have some quality, something intangible, discernible to my eyes only. Women who gave you their everything one day yet still had something more the next, that was the kind of woman I sought. I admired Judith because we got on well together, talked like old friends, and shared treasured secrets. She paid for our trip to Mayreau, we took in Bequia and Palm Island, she drove me to the rocky Owia Salt Pond on the windward side of SVG. Fancying a fish broth one Sunday, she hired a taxi to Layou to buy fresh red snapper.

Whatever she fancied she got. In return she took time off work to 'care' for me, as she put it, for I was her 'sailor-man'. Each trip ended with a parcel of books to read at sea, before we departed there would be a large ping-wing basket with a meal to savour on board, a quart of rum, and a selection of my favourite fruits. Someone had to look after me, she would say, without *her* care, a sailor like me 'could easily fall overboard and drown'.

I looked forward to our trips, I have to admit. For each place we visited she had some curious historical fact to titillate. We did the mainland, and most of the Grenadines. She arranged all this for us, but I steadfastly kept one secret from her. After each trip I vowed to confess to her that I was from SVG too, that I grew up in Fancy, that I had been a primary school teacher in Bequia: but I didn't have the heart. And the longer it went on the harder it became.

Out in the Atlantic or Caribbean Sea, on wondrous star-filled nights, under the influence of a cooling sea breeze, a lazy tide or a warm rum, men only, sailor-life was the best in the world. We were a mixed crew on the *SS Jestina*. There were men from Grenada, Barbados, Martinique, Barbados, St Kitts and Trinidad, our ranks included Verrol St Elmo, a former Leewards Islands cricketer, Hale Burke, an upcoming calypsonian, and Festus Naire, a disgraced police sergeant from Belize. Dabriel, from St Lucia was pure East Indian, Budowe, of Barbados, who, like me, bruised his arms in lifting the lightest crate, of Scottish descent. Quiet, but fearless during the fiercest storm, Cup-a-Joe, a Carib from Martinique, told stories he couldn't recall the following day.

We were a mixed bunch, then, the Caribbean with its exotic combination of South America, Africa, India and Europe. On nights when only the clucking of the engine and the silky parting of the sea disturbed the quiet, the men boasted of recent conquests. I was a listener, for there were always those with a higher quotient in looks, build and conquests, and I've never believed in betraying a woman's 'inside business'.

At thirty-seven, one of the youngest on board, I naturally deferred to the men of experience. They knew personally the history of each Caribbean island from Tobago to Cuba, between them they had explored the 83 000 square miles of Guyana. I listened, enthralled, but seldom joined in. 'Creole girls,' Hilton

Bowman suggested one night before we staggered wearily to our bunks, 'fellas, when you go ashore tomorrow, find yourself a beautiful Caribbean woman. Young or old, pretty or plain, but willing, fill her up to the brim with kindness: discover the reason why we sailors are able to put up with weeks at sea.'

Hilton was good. Lanky, sinewy and strong, he could unload his share of freight in half the time I took. When we got round to women there was no doubting his pedigree either. The night he danced four women simultaneously at a club in Dominica - one at the front, one behind, one with the left arm, one with the right - kept us amused, and in awe, after many a hard day. Others could be encouraged to boast, but when it came to women I kept their secrets all to myself. For how could I tell them about Judith? What could I say about a black woman who saw herself above others because of her hair and features?

Whenever we docked in SVG Judith was there early. Wearing an A-line skirt or slacks, a broad smile on her face, she would wait at the gate, clasping our picnic lunch for the day. Exhausted from lifting and ferrying crates and boxes, she could sum up my mood at once. She let me sleep to recover, she soothed me when I woke up. Here at last was a woman who understood this sailor's need for rest. She would try to make me laugh, biting my lip until it hurt and giggling at my pain. 'Close your eyes,' she would order me as we kissed, and when I did, she would nibble my ear, honk my nose or exhale noisily into my mouth. Mixing childishness and knowing, every time I thought of giving her up, some silly gesture of hers would win me over.

Where her obsession with her skin came from I couldn't fathom. She knew how much it annoyed me yet she was forever placing her arm next to mine and saying, 'Your hand about the same complexion as mine.' When she spoke of her relatives it was, 'Andrea is from the dark side of the family,' or, 'My sisters better-looking than me, but I'm the fairest.' In time I learned to ignore her, for her other qualities more than compensated for this slight irritation.

But I continued to resist meeting her family. I made excuses, lied about having to return to the ship, or promised to talk about it on my next visit. When she begged me I felt bad. But what kind of life could I offer her? Why make promises I couldn't keep?

'Don't fool women,' was Hilton's constant advice. 'Don't fool them, and don't fool yourself either. The women latch onto you because you just land in their territory, they like a good time, and if you lucky they might give you a good time too. But just remember: most of them have their man at home: to them a sailor-boy is just a bit of sport. So don't fool them, oblige them like they oblige you, and leave it at that.' Despite her insistence about her complexion, despite her infatuation with her looks, I found myself breaking this rule with Judith. For I was slowly developing feelings for her.

For two years we corresponded, met, and picked up our half-finished conversations. That she looked forward to my leave was obvious, and I began to spend the long nights at sea thinking of her, wondering what she was up, visualising her entertaining a group of tourists at the base of the Soufriere volcano, at the Botanic Gardens or Fort Charlotte. The more I resisted, heaving at the tug rope, the firmer she pulled me in.

Her obsessions began to appear unimportant, childish

notions she would one day discard. Something was definitely changing in me, I began to disobey my own rules. When, one Saturday, the crew descended on a new bar in Antigua and I remained on board with Burke learning to play the guitar, I knew I was in deep trouble.

One Wednesday lunchtime, by *Laynes* in Middle Street, Kingstown, Judith introduced me to her brother, Saunders and a sister, Louise. Later that day Palna, her eldest sister, barged in on us at *Henry's* restaurant in Vermont, seven miles from Kingstown on the leeward side. Just coincidence, Judith whispered unconvincingly when she noticed me frowning, it was just one of those days. The three of us had lunch, Palna sparkling while Judith fretted as though she feared her sister would reveal some deep secret to me. I studied them carefully without making it too obvious, saw the family resemblance, heard the similarities in their laughter.

They looked alike, they shared the same hearty appetites and love of cocktails. An hour later, well fed and watered, Palna rose to return to her job at the Marketing Board in Kingstown. Confident of her sister's discretion, or having downed three cocktails also, Judith had stopped worrying by then. 'So good to see you Palna, sis,' she sang to Palna, giving her a big hug, 'we must have lunch again sometime, the two brown-skin girls.' She said this in the girlish voice she occasionally used when we were alone and she wanted to play. I took her invitation as an attempt at a joke, but Palna wasn't amused. 'Black,' she swiftly corrected Judith, wriggling from her grasp and giving her a cold stare, 'there's only one brown-skin girl here: and is not me!'

Later that rainy night, in the tiny room Judith had rented for us at Corbeaux Town, three miles from her home, we reflected on what Palna might say to the family. I sensed that Judith had invited her sister to force my hand and told her so. She firmly denied it but I wasn't sure I believed her. Either way I didn't really care. She was twenty-eight, a woman, no one could make me do what I didn't want to. It was just after nine, the night cooled by a light drizzle. The room was small, with a tiny bed. Judith was sitting on the bed, so I took a wooden chair and sat by the window.

It had been a month since our last meeting. The letters had continued, getting longer, more intimate, and increasingly desperate. I was seriously considering meeting her family, I wrote, loading and unloading ships left too many sores that took weeks to heal. Now, the incident with Palna forgotten, she was about to perform for me as she usually did on my first day back.

She began by carefully removing the clip at the back of her head to release her hair. The black mass uncurled and descended tantalisingly to her shoulders. Gathering the two extremities she lifted it gently so that she could apply a dash of perfume at the nape of the neck. I watched her and smiled. As my heart quickened she unzipped the simple, light-blue cotton dress, a slight fumble with the zip adding to the tension within me. Manoeuvring the dress over the shoulders, left first, then the right, she shimmied her waist to lower the dress until, at half mast, she could climb out of it.

Judith wasn't a woman to rush. Time was always on her side. With great care she folded the dress then placed it on the bed. Removing the beer from my hand, she placed it on the window ledge, then lowered herself onto my lap. I held her by the waist and squeezed her. Her body was soft and welcoming. Wearing the black lingerie set I had posted her a month previously, memories of our first night in Kingstown came flooding back.

'See, Neil,' she said, 'you like?'

'I like very much,' I admitted, for they fitted her perfectly.

'I tried them on soon as I get them, but tonight is the first night I wear them.'

'You lie,' I said, playfully, squeezing her again, drawing her closer to me, and kissing her on the lips. 'I know you.'

'What happen, you don't believe me?' she asked, a touch annoyed, missing the intended flippancy of my comment.

'Whatever you tell me I believe,' I said, stroking her right arm to atone for my crassness.

'That's not what I ask you: I ask if you believe me.'

'Yes, Judith, I believe you: I believe tonight is the first night you wear the set.'

'Say it like you mean it.'

'What, you doubting me? I ever lie to you?'

'You don't lie, you just don't tell the truth.'

'I do.'

'No you don't.'

'Give me one example where I tell you a lie.'

'You write and say I'm the only woman in your life but you still refuse to come home for me.'

'Oh that.'

'Yes *that*. How do you think that make me feel?'

'So what you doing here tonight then? If you feel so strong about it why you still with me?'

At this point I began to feel that the conversation was running

14

away from me. From both of us in fact. It had been a particularly choppy crossing from Barbados, I was bruised and tired. This wasn't the night to drag up these matters: her company, her arms, and a long restful sleep were what I longed for.

'Because, Neil,' she said, with a seriousness that caught me off guard, 'because I promised to wait for you and I'm the kind of woman who knows how to keep a promise. You might have your fun in the islands but that isn't me. I make a pledge, I keep it. You don't realise what I go through for you. You don't really appreciate me.'

'Of course I appreciate you Judith. But I sail: the Caribbean Sea and Atlantic Ocean are my home. That is how it was when we first meet, that is how it is this Wednesday. I see you what, ten times a year for a few days at a time, we have a nice time together, you are the best company a man can have: but sailing is my life.'

'But you can't live at sea forever: sooner or later you have to realise that: you want me to be there for you?'

'How long you prepared to wait?'

'Until you ready to settle down.'

'Judith, you're young,' I said, saying the first thing that came into my head, for I hadn't expected this and didn't have the energy for clear thinking. 'You have to do what is best for you. I don't work to months and years.'

'I don't mind waiting.'

'Put you first Judith,' I said, 'look after yourself.'

'But we get on so well and we so close now. You need me, that's what you say in all your letters, and is the same with me: unless is pretend you pretending the whole time!'

'Whatever I write I mean.'

'That is why I cast everything else aside: so I can be there when you outgrow the sea.'

'But you might have to wait a long time.'

'A year, two years, three, whatever it take is fine by me.'

'You will do that for me?'

'Yes.'

'But why?'

'Because I made a promise. I used to think that every man was wrong for me, but that was before I meet you.'

'Judith, look at me, look carefully, pick the beam out of your eyes: when you stare at Neil Pope what you see? A man you can settle down with, or a man to take in small doses?'

'I don't want you bit by bit any longer, is the total man I want.'

'But you don't truly know me Judith: and I don't know you either. I met you in a bar, I can't give up my life for a woman I pick up in bar!'

'You didn't pick me up,' she protested vehemently, 'I don't frequent bars. I was there with some friends because that is where we sometimes go after work. I just happen to be there that night. I'm not one of those women who see the gold of *El Dorado* whenever a ship dock from Martinique. I work for the Tourist Board, Neil, I get a fair wage, I like to eat out, I like rum and coke and cocktails, and a lively dance to finish off the evening: don't say I ever tell you or show you different. I don't lie to you, lying never get a person anywhere.'

'Why I should believe you?'

'Because you don't have a choice: when you think carefully about it, neither of us have a choice: I have to believe you when you say you don't enjoy going ashore anymore, and you have to take my word that I don't fool around.'

'You make things seem so simple.'

'That is because when you look close, they *are* simple.'

'Nothing simple with you, Judith, you complicate everything. You not happy unless you get noticed, you think you're better than other women because of your hair and your complexion. I don't like that, Judith.'

'Well soon you won't have a choice, you going to have to accept me for what I am.'

'Why is that?'

'Because I think I might be pregnant.'

'What did you say?' I asked, my heart starting to thump.

The talk of settling down, the promises to wait, made sense now. It was too much to take in. My head began to spin, my ears began to filter the sounds of the night, amplifying the chirping of the crickets. I could feel the blood spurting through the veins in my temples and forehead.

'I think I'm making a baby,' she said.

'Why you didn't tell me before?'

My heart had settled down, but my skin was burning up. I looked at her face and saw her now, not as the woman in the bar, or the obsessive, but as a mother-to-be. I was scared, terrified. I didn't know what to do or say.

'Because I wanted to surprise you,' she answered, with a tenderness that touched my heart.

I kissed her. I squeezed her tight and asked, 'You sure?'

'Yes: we going to have a beautiful baby girl.'

I kissed her again.

'Judith, you sure-sure?'

'Yes Neil, I'm sure. And I know is going to be a girl.'

'How can you tell?'

'I just know, I can feel it.'

'How?'

'Don't ask me. This might be my first time but I know I'm not wrong.'

'I hope so,' I said, truthfully, 'I really hope is a beautiful baby girl.'

'And she going to be just like me and you,' she said. 'She's going to be a nice brown-skin baby with long straight hair and brown eyes.'

'Judith,' I said, softly, for she risked ruining the moment, 'she' s going to be a black baby.'

'How could she be black when she is *our* baby?'

'Because both of us black.'

'My grandfather was Irish, my father is half-, my baby going to be the same as me, with the same eyes and hair.'

'Get up Judith,' I said, the good news soured, 'get up, put on your clothes and drive me back to town.'

'Why Neil? Why?'

'Just get up!' I said, forcing her out of my lap.

The rain had eased but the dampness hung in the air. Along the narrow road from Mespo to Kingstown, up steep hills and down, Judith drove slowly, the headlights disappearing in dark valleys and reappearing suddenly on the bough of tall trees. With the windows down, the swishing of the tyres punctuated our silence. As we drove in the darkness I had visions of Judith refusing to receive a black baby, of her haring from the hospital with the midwife in pursuit with the little bundle.

Joey's bar kept coming back to me. Our crazy dancing, the endless cocktails, escorting her to her car after midnight. Who had done the choosing, I asked myself, had I picked Judith, or did she make the move? I didn't have the answer and it didn't matter now. She was pregnant, she clung to the idea that her tangled ancestry wasn't as sordid as everyone else's: how could I give up my life for a woman like that?

Exaggerating the concentration needed to navigate the tight corners and negotiate the sheer drops, Judith rarely looked to her left where I was sipping a petit of *Sunset* rum and wishing I had never met her, praying I was back in my tiny bunk on the *SS Jestina*. I had nothing to say to her now, we had become strangers.

When we arrived in Kingstown she asked, 'Neil, what we going to do?'

'I know what *I'm* going to do,' I replied, 'what about you?'

'I'm going to have the baby.'

'I know that,' I said, 'I mean afterwards.'

'I was hoping you would be there to support me: but look like I was wrong.'

'I'll support the baby, you don't have to worry about that.'

'And what about me? I don't need support?'

'You don't need support, Judith, you need help.'

'Then help me, Neil.'

'I can't help you: you have to help yourself.'

I opened the door and got out of the car. I closed it softly and took a final look at her. There was a sadness about her eyes, but I had recognised that from the beginning. The anxiety and helplessness behind the sparkle weren't my doing. 'Goodbye, Judith,' I said, and began the journey through the town.

By any measure, Kingstown is small. Beautiful by night, compact, to see the harbour from Sion Hill or Fort Charlotte at sunrise is to recognise that there is beauty even in small things. I walked from Frenches to Bay Street, slowly, with no destination in mind. I needed some sea air to clear my head, I needed time to think.

Turning right at the wharf, I heard the soft rippling of the sea, saw the outline of the vessels in the harbour and smelled the gasoline of the tethered ships. The town had truly gone to sleep, only insomniac sailors and dancing women were still on their feet.

For twenty minutes I walked until I arrived at *Joey's*. I sat on a stool outside, listening to the laughter and music. The dampness and heat made the bar attractive, the smell of rum invited me in, the music also. But I wasn't ready. I wasn't in the mood for celebrations. Only when it started to rain and my head had cleared, did I go in to join my shipmates.

I strolled directly to the bar, ordered a large rum and downed it in one go. I ordered another, took a swig and, seeing Burke in a corner, his guitar on the chair beside him, I went over. I commandeered the guitar and strummed it vigorously. The words of a song came to me so I stood up, demanded 'Attention!' and began to sing.

> *Brown-skin girl, stay home and mind baby*
> *Brown-skin girl, stay home and mind baby*
> *I'm going away, on a sailing boat*
> *And if I don't come back*
> *Stay home and mind baby*

A few people quickly latched onto the chorus so we sang, at the top of our voices:

Brown-skin girl, stay home and mind baby
Brown-skin girl, stay home and mind baby
I'm going away, on a sailing boat
And if I don't come back
Stay home and mind baby

Just as quickly as they had picked it up the others abandoned the song and returned to their drinking, dropping out one by one, so that after a while, leaning against the bar, I was left strumming miserably. No one was noticing me now, I was simply another intoxicated sailor, bitter, stupid, who had disobeyed the code and allowed himself to be ensnared by a woman.

Her dress soaked through, her precious hair a sorry black tangle, I was returning the guitar to Burke when Judith emerged from a dark corner of the bar. She looked a wreck. The light cotton dress clung crookedly to her, she dragged herself along as though her feet were made of lead. She grabbed at my arm, tried to ask for an explanation. But I evaded her and staggered out into Bay Street.

'Neil!' I heard her pleading, as I made for the ship. 'Neil, stop! Neil wait!'

But I didn't. For what was there to say to her?

I vowed not to go back to SVG after that. Whenever our vessel was due there, I asked for a transfer. Northwest to Haiti, Jamaica and Cuba, or to the South American coast to Guyana, I got to know the entire Caribbean, not as a sailor, but as a man, determined to see the countries in daylight. The final Friday of each month I posted half my wages to Judith. Her swift replies I refused to open. A large pile of white envelopes marked *Urgent* remained at the bottom of my suitcase.

But on stormy nights, or when it was calm, I often wondered about the child, and how Judith was. I wanted to see them, but knew that, however much we are tempted, we cannot rewrite the past. Hilton had married and returned to land, Burke had hung up his guitar and become a ship's engineer. When the men gathered on deck after a hard day, I remained in my bunk staring blankly at the sea or listening to the gentle vibration of the ship.

Those days! Those glory days! There was a time when missing a 'landing' cost a crew member a bottle of Haitian rum. When, unless you were sick or lame, refusal to go ashore meant waltzing on deck for ten minutes with a box of bananas for a partner in front of the other men. I didn't care for such things now. I had no idea what I wanted.

After seven months, in October, I returned to the island. Clutching my small suitcase, I surveyed the familiar harbour before beginning the slow walk to the shore. It was early in the day but already quite warm. I ambled past the palm trees evenly spaced along the long arc of the car park, noticed the red and white flowers of the *Jump-up-and-kiss-me* sprouting in the loose black sand at the base of the trees. A taxi pulled up beside me as I neared the gate. I accepted gratefully and climbed in.

The driver was in his early sixties, with short spiky black hair like iron filings, and solid arms.

'Where to?' he asked, as we left the wharf.

'A hotel,' I answered.

'Which one?'

'I used to stay at one in Harmony Hall,' I confessed, feeling a bit of a fool for not knowing, 'but I don't remember the name.'

'*The Ravina?*' he suggested. 'Good choice. Lots of tourists stay there and they have nothing for it but praise. It's a bit expensive though.'

'That's not a problem.'

'What line of work you in?' he asked, when the price didn't put me off.

'I sail.'

'Pay well, then?'

'The money not bad.'

'What about the work?'

'Hard: I don't know how much longer I can keep going.'

It was like this for the duration of the journey. From Kingstown to Harmony Hall he probed, like man seeking a change of occupation. At last, after thirty-five minutes, the taxi clambered up a steep hill and pulled up in front of the building, carefully avoiding a pack of welcoming puppies. The driver carried my bags to the reception, accepted my ten-dollar tip, and wished me an enjoyable stay. I booked in, ordered an early lunch, and went upstairs to my room.

After a spell at sea there is nothing more satisfying than a long leisurely shower to wash away the dirt and smell of the ship. The cuts and grazes that are a part of the job soothed, the salt and wood cleansed from the system, I felt refreshed. A white cotton vest and khaki shorts took my fancy after I had greased and combed my short hair. Five minutes later, I was lying on the bed waiting for lunch to be delivered when there was a knock at the door. Too lazy to get up I shouted, 'Come in.'

There was no response to this so I repeated the suggestion, but louder this time. Still no response. Assuming that the waiter had his hands full with the tray, I got up, sauntered to the door and turned the handle. I wasn't prepared for what I saw. For an instant I stood there, unable to speak.

'Judith,' I stuttered, when I eventually found words, 'what you doing here?'

Judith didn't answer. I stared at her and, in return, her stony gaze didn't miss an inch of my body. After a short, awkward interval I stepped aside to let her enter. I waited for a moment, closed the door and followed her in.

'Judith!' I said again, as she gazed at the sea, the outline of Bequia visible in the distance. 'Well?'

She didn't answer straight away. In her own time she said, in a gruff voice, 'What?'

'What you doing here?' I repeated. 'How's the baby?'

'The baby is fine,' she replied in a tone that didn't mask her irritation at my question.

Slowly, very slowly, she turned to face me. She was wearing a white blouse with fat square buttons and a brown pencil skirt that appeared a size too big. Her figure had gone, she was thin and shapeless, the brightness of her eyes had dimmed. Casting her tired eyes over me, assessing me as she had at the door, she shook her head several times in what seemed a verdict of hopelessness.

A silence followed during which she concentrated at the wooden floor as though she had forgotten the reason for the visit. Stumbling over the dozens of questions in my mind, I finally asked, 'Where's the baby? Is it a boy or a girl?'

'Girl,' she muttered, as though I wasn't worth wasting words on.

'How is she?'

'The baby is fine.'

'Where is she?'

'Why you want to know?'

'Because I do.'

'Why you interested now, after all this time?'

'I send you half my wages every month, you don't call that interest?'

'Money is nothing Neil, nothing! Your money is nothing.'

'I would like to see her.'

'What you would like is *your* problem: I can't solve your problems for you.'

'I just want to see her.'

'Is not "her", she has a name.'

'What's her name?'

'Juneil,' Judith said, and for the first time her voice softened. 'Her name is Juneil.'

'What's she like?' I asked, trying to picture her in my mind, the way I had so many times at sea especially when the waves lashed the boat, when we pitched from crest to watery trough, and I wondered who would weep for me should we capsize.

'She's a beautiful girl,' her voice was soft and emotional.

A feeling of shame descended on me. For what I had done, for what I hadn't. I longed to see her, to sorry for not coming sooner.

'Eight months, Neil,' Judith said, as I covered my eyes with my left palm, 'I write to you twice a month, not a word coming back. Every ship that dock I was down by the gate waiting. Didn't your friends tell you? Did they report back on the mad woman under her parasol with her baby? I bet you had a good laugh at my expense: silly Judith, eh, stupid Judith, staying home to mind baby!'

'Judith, I'm sorry,' I said. 'The song: I don't know where it came from. I didn't mean it, I must have been drunk.'

I felt like a coward, a weakling. I should have told her how strongly I disapproved of her obsession with her colour, should have replied to her letters. I walked over to her and placed a hand on her right shoulder. She didn't react, didn't flinch from my touch. With a cold stare, but without her previous disdain, she contemplated the man before her.

'It doesn't matter now,' she answered, coldly, ' I looked after her when you were far away. When you had the opportunity to come and see her, you didn't make the effort. You can be as sorry as you like.'

I left my arm on her shoulder.

'You can't just drift into her life when you want, Neil,' she continued. 'You can't turn up after a year and expect us to receive you like the prodigal son!'

'She's my daughter, Judith,' I pleaded, 'you can't deny me that. I wanted to come and see her but I couldn't.'

'What was stopping you?'

'You. You Judith, you were the problem. I used to love being with you, but I can't take a woman who doesn't like what she is. How could I be with a woman who is so ashamed of her colour when she look in the mirror black turn to brown?'

Judith eased herself from my touch and sat on the bed. I remained standing.

'So you abandon your child because of me?' she asked, her voice lacking its earlier harshness.

'I didn't abandon her,' I replied, 'I'll never abandon her.'

'But you're prepared to give *me* up?'

'What has to be has to be, Judith. Is not my choice.'

'Whose choice is it then?'

'Yours.'

'How could it be mine?'

'I can't sacrifice everything I work for for someone obsessed with their features and their complexion.'

'People can change, you know,' she suggested, her conciliatory tone coming as a surprise to me.

'Can *you*?' I asked.

She didn't reply. Instead, to my surprise, she got up and headed for the door.

'Not even a goodbye then?' I asked as she turned the handle.

She hesitated. A shadow of the woman who had captivated me, dark circles about the eyes, her skin soft and slack, she had dropped the walk, she was as ordinary now as I was.

'You really want to see Juneil?' she asked after an interval, 'you genuinely want to see her?'

'Yes,' I replied, 'yes, I do.'

The door was ajar. She remained standing in the doorway, her back to me. Two minutes later I heard footsteps. They grew louder and louder until, before long, there were four of us in the room. Her face as solemn as a judge, her sister Palna, kissed the baby on the lips and offered her to me.

The child's hair was in dozens of tiny plaits. Her hair and skin glistened from a generous application of coconut oil. Her eyes were the brightest black I had ever seen, her skin soft and a silky black. I kissed her on the forehead. She wriggled in my arms, her tiny feet landing in my stomach. I kissed her again and she began to cry.

I passed her over to Judith, carefully, like precious cargo. The absentee parent, I accepted her totally. She was real, lively, I had no intention of leaving her again. But Judith: how did her mother see her, an undeniably black baby? Did she accept her, or had she passed the responsibility to Palna who had brought Juneil to me?

I observed Judith closely. I saw the tender look in her eyes, the intimate bond between mother and child.

'She's a strange,' Judith said, addressing me directly, 'she cries when you feed her, she cries when you plait her hair. She screams when she's on her tummy, it's blue murder if she's on her back. She's a wonderful child.'

'She's beautiful,' I agreed. 'She's wonderful.'

'Thank you,' said Judith.

I looked at her and saw not the woman of that night at *Joey's*, out to impress with her stylish walk, but settled now, content to be what she was. Her clothes were plain and ordinary, she wore no makeup, her hair, parted down the middle, had been constructed into two fat plaits. I had certainly changed and so had she. I watched her straighten the child's dress and tidy one of the curls that had unwound. There was no doubting her acceptance of the child.

'Would you like to meet my father?' she asked.

I thought back to my promise never to go along this route, but what are promises for?

'No problem,' I replied, with a shrug of the shoulders.

She went to the door, signalled, and a few minutes later, the taxi driver entered the room. He was well-built and tall. He smiled at me as though he had tricked me in a card game. I looked at Palna and Judith to my left, and saw their anxiety. I knew what I had to do. I wasn't intimidated, no one could force me to do what I didn't want to.

I offered my hand to Mr Neverson, he nodded in appreciation, and we shook.

'There's no need to stay in a hotel, you know, ' he said, still holding my hand. 'Why not come home with us?'

I thought about it. Not long, but long enough.

'Why not?' I replied. 'Why not?'

business is business

In September 1967, my nineteenth birthday two months behind me, I become the youngest businessman in SVG. For three frenetic weeks, the shirts I sell make me so famous, what seem like the entire country form a trail to my humble front door in Biabou. No exaggeration. Tailors arrive to ask my advice and, imagine that, a department store in the capital even send their big man to negotiate with me! Who couldn't afford car travel by foot, a fella from Troumaka make the journey on a bike, arriving when the moon undressing for the night. From leeward to town to country, 'Cool Fit' shirts cause such a stir, no body could afford to be without one!

Before my meteoric rise, my acquaintance with clothes - my three nylon shirts, my green shorts and work trousers, and not forgetting my yellow merino - hang lazily in a tiny wardrobe in the tiny bedroom of my parents' tiny house. Linen, wool, cotton, if you lay out a garment before me at the time and ask me to describe the material, or to name it, would be guess I guessing, no point in lying.

A white shirt to wear to work, a white shirt to wear home, and a white shirt to lime in, I follow my father's dress code completely. I make sure my shirt match my trousers, I particular not to leave home without a belt. If a man in an accident accused of dirty shoes or grubby fingernails, then that man definitely not me, I assure my father.

All short sleeved, same colour and design, and same length - identical in every way, then - people whisper and give me funny looks, like they do in villages everywhere, when they realise my preference for white shirts. Those who study me coming and going, wondering how I manage to look suave seven days a week nudge each other and giggle, but I know better than to take them on.

White match the smoothness of my black skin, white set off my chocolate-brown work trousers, the shorts I favour at weekends not bad with it either. Who want to gawp at me only wasting their eyes, I tell myself as I go about my business with my head held high. But when Naba Glasgow accost me one evening and accuse me of owning *one* shirt which I try to pass as three, the effrontery force me to react.

For I was waiting for the idle vagabond. Permanently shirtless, an oversized boy who pass his day patrolling the village, gazing at the sea, or counting the number of ripe breadfruit on each tree, he lambast me one time too often.

'Remind me who spend two years in every single class in primary school,' I say to him as we queuing up to buy sprats later that evening. 'Who leave school at twenty-five, when all their friends already raising family?'

I watch him raise the back of his left hand to his mouth in shock like a child who allow a bottle of *JuC* to slip through his fingers. His eyes bulge, his lips start to tremble theatrically.

'Eldon Duvalle,' he reply in a soft voice for effect, 'so I leave primary school at eighteen, so what? At least I don't wash my *one* shirt overnight and iron it in the morning and think I can fool the village!'

I pelt the blow, it sting, but, accustomed to insults, he always have an answer ready. People titter, so I walk slowly away from the fish van, my bowl empty, butter-bread for my evening meal instead of fried sprats.

Thinking about it later that night, I could understand where Naba get the idea. At the time, a few months before my rise to fame, I was working as 'Security' in Mr Gatherer's shop in Choppins. Not the most lucrative job, of course, but other fellas from the village selling exotic figs, succulent maugh-faugh-baugh, copra, forbidden, tomatoes, and mangoes, and just about scratching a living. Farming not in my blood, so imagine the pittance I would make if I try to compete with them! Security more my line, I decide, 'inside' work preferable to baking in the hot sun day after day and struggling to sell your goods.

During their lunchtime children from the local primary used to invade Mr Gatherer's shop for crush cakes, sandwiches and heavy bread, and one or two get the impression that they could stuff a bag of sweets or a marble in their pocket for every glass of mauby or cake they buy. For five dollars a week, my task was to upend them, turn out their pockets and chase them back to school, an extra fifty cents on my salary and all the bread pudding I could eat if I could persuade them to buy some stationery before they leave.

So, as you can see, the job not too taxing. For me was just a stepping stone to my real ambition, the police force. Nanton Buller, who sign up two years earlier, already gain a stripe at Calliaqua Police Station for placating a madman who claim that a neighbour dog posting letters to his cat, letters *he* had to collect at the post office every day for his gorgeous Tibby, and reply to. If a slow-witted and lethargic boy like Nanton could bring off an arrest, I tell myself, I know I was in with more than a good chance.

For then, as now, police was the cosiest job in SVG. Even teaching couldn't beat it. My application was in, I had the size, but I was no good at drinking rum, and I didn't want to bring the force into disrepute because of this.

While on the beat, a good friend inform me, a constable have to get his book signed at three different places. A welcome rest and a chat with the priest in the shade at the local church, a complimentary ice cream at the gas station, ten minutes discussing the times tables with the headmistress in the local primary school, and a constable complete his daily duty. The signatures prove that he getting around, doing his bit to becalm criminals. I used to see Sergeant Wilkins in the village at midday, imperiously dressed, not a whisper of sweat on him, and I conclude that was the life for me. Cycling from village to village, returning to barracks to play cards and dominoes, I had the bulk, it was just a matter of time, beer and rum, before I in the ranks too.

Out of habit, at that age, I rise early each morning for a run on the black sandy beach at Shipping Bay. My feet sinking into the hot sand, my calves throbbing, I don't feel right if I don't extend myself, snatching a dip in the sea afterwards before the sun fully awake. One Sunday, on the walk home from my morning session, a man stop me at the foot of the hill leading to Spring.

The man was tall, burly, with a gentle, smiling face. Dressed in a green shirt with a red handkerchief in the breast pocket, brown shoes, yellow socks and white trousers, looking as though he on the way to carnival, he break down, he say, apologetically, for forty minutes he trying to start the wretched vehicle, but no luck. He have a boat to catch, he add, he in a perilous position because he don't know anything about cars.

That made two of us, but I wasn't going to tell him that. In my experience, fellas in possession of that amount of ignorance usually worth helping, so I promise to assist, nodding confidently, as though fixing vehicles was an everyday thing with me. I usher him gently out the way and slide into the driver's seat. Cocking my head to the left, I turn the ignition and listen. Nothing. I cock my head to the right, a look of deep concentration on my face, and try again. Still nothing. I turn a couple of switches, the wipers and indicators flicker then die. The man give me a funny look, as if he doubt my credentials. I smile to assure him I have things under control. I press the brake, clutch and accelerator, listen to them squeak, then declare haughtily, 'The battery low: lift the bonnet.'

Between us, between twenty and thirty minutes later, we locate the latch and get the bonnet up. I tug at the battery, twist it, shake it, jerk the wires and nod to him like a nurse loading an injection.

'Try that,' I suggest. 'Try she now.'

To my amazement the car burst into life! The engine stutter then begin to whine. The man rev the engine, pressing the accelerator to the floor several times as if he need to hear and feel the rattling to convince himself the car not going to change its mind and pass out again. After he satisfy, he switch off the motor, climb out, and place a grateful arm on my shoulder. He smile at me and, hands in my pockets, I smile back. Wait here, he say, as if I going anywhere, I have something for you. Ducking into the back of the car, he produce a garment in a plastic wrapper and offer it to me. Was a shirt, a fine check, of delicate blue and green.

'Take this,' he say. 'You don't know it, but you just rescue a businessman.'

'Thanks,' I reply, accepting the package, 'what line of business you in?'

'I sell clothes,' he answer. 'Trousers, belts, shirts, shoes, frocks, petticoats, stockings, panties: anything you want I can supply.'

I can't place his accent. One moment he sound English, the next Trinidadian, in between I detect a trace of American, and a large dose of Vincy.

'Where you from?' I enquire.

'Antigua,' he reply. 'But my business based in Dominica. I travel the Caribbean selling clothes at affordable prices. See the shirts in the back of the car? I sell over five hundred of these in Kingstown already, but I'm just giving the shops in the countryside the opportunity to make a profit too.'

'The shirts look nice,' I agree, for any shirt with a bit of colour couldn't be all bad, especially when it free. 'Where they made?'

'What's your name, young man?' he ask, as if he about to lecture me on the dangers of swimming on the windward coast, or to respect your parents and teachers.

'Eldon Duvalle.'

'Now, Eldon,' he say, 'you ever hear about commerce?'

'No,' I answer. 'They never teach us that in secondary school. We only learn reading, writing, arithmetic and history. Oh, and enough biology to put us off sex.'

'Well,' he whisper, 'I going to teach you the basics. Right here, right now, and I won't charge you a cent. Secondary school or not, take it from me, is a simple concept. Businesses sell, customers buy. Customers demand, businesses supply. You still with me?'

It sound simple, my curiosity aroused. 'You think I could become a businessman?'

The man look me over slowly from head to toe. He scratch his chin, then nod approvingly like a preacher about to accept a stray sheep into his flock.

'You have the demeanour,' he say, and as he nod and grin, I could swear I recognise his face from a dance in Arnos Vale in February that flop so bad the promoter had to seek refuge in a nearby church. 'But in business you have to look and sound good, and you have to believe in your product. Most of all you have to titillate the customer. If you make a small investment with me, you could quickly learn about accumulation and speculation. Your money could compound at least 300 per cent!'

I watch him, an enormous man, stuffed with words, handsome, with even, white teeth, hardly a bead of sweat on him in the morning heat, and imagine becoming like him. His nails in good condition - the mark of a good man, according to my father - and although his accent change country with every sentence, I can't help but like him.

'Tell me about the shirts,' I say, for I want to hear more.

'They are the finest on this island, or on any island in the Caribbean for that matter. They are English shirts, handmade, built to last, warm in winter, cool in summer. The finest fabrics used in their making, synthetic and natural combining to produce a combustible garment.'

'How much they selling for?' I ask.

'In pounds, even *I* couldn't afford one, and neither could you. But in dollars, ten.'

'Ten dollars?'

'Five, if you purchase the entire stock in the car.'

'How many is that?'

'One hundred shirts.'

'I don't have five hundred dollars.'

'How much you have?'

'I have one hundred save, and I know where my mother hide another hundred.'

'Good.' A broad smile appear on the man's face. 'You obviously possess the businessman's acumen: you decisive, but most of all you have the ability to raise funds at a stroke.'

'Really?'

'Nobody ever tell you?'

'No.'

The man place his hands on my shoulders again and, facing me, he begin to massage my collar bones.

'Well, believe me, Eldon, you have. It's in your eyes, your talk, every part of you exude business.'

He drop me home and, after turning the house upside down, I muster up a hundred and fifty dollars. And now my wardrobe full of shirts. Eldon Duvalle on the way to becoming a businessman!

In the late sixties, Sunday was 'theatre' day. The cinema in Georgetown specialise in westerns, Tarzan films, horror, biblical epics, any movie but romance. The audience roar with laughter or derision, they shout instructions to the actors, they divulge the plot after the second reel. But first you have to get a ticket.

Fifty cents for a seat in 'pit', a precarious few yards from the screen, seventy-five cents for the stalls, a dollar for the comfort of balcony, to obtain a ticket was a task for weightlifters, six-footers, and those people who feel the day wasted if they don't get or give a bruise. I used to watch the scramble, the pushing, kicking and shoving of the buyers, trousers dripping with sweat, shirt torn from their back, and feel ashamed. Now, dressed in my fine English shirt, I pass my fifty cents to Mac Charles and stand well away to watch the fight for tickets.

'Cool Fit', the shirt really live up to its name. In the heat of the Sunday afternoon, on the bus journey to Georgetown, it filter the heat effortlessly like a net curtain. But it cling to my skin where I sweat, so I unbutton it to allow the air through. My friends look at me as we watch The Ten Commandments, no longer the boy in white, and I see the surprise and jealously in their face. Each time they attempt to touch the shirt I fend them off with a, 'Don't touch what you can't buy!' As we drive home in the cool evening they feverish with excitement. Cool Fit? They have to have one too!

The next morning, while I about to leave for my session at the beach, two of them, Pancil Jacobs and Man-Dorothy, block me in the porch. Which store in Kingstown selling the shirts, they demand to know, how much they cost? I invite them into my room, open the wardrobe, and watch their eyes almost bolt out of the sockets.

'What happen, you turn criminal?' Man-Dorothy ask.

'The clothes wash up on the beach?' Pancil want to know.

'I set up in business,' I explain, 'I selling shirts.'

'If they make you look so sharp,' Man-Dorothy almost hoarse with excitement, 'imagine how they will look on me!'

'That's because they handmade,' I tell them. 'They made from a new fabric developed in England.'

'Dacron?' Man-Dorothy ask, unable to stand still, because he was a man who follow fashion.

I shake my head.

'Polyester?' Pancil ask, almost salivating at the word.

I shake my head again. 'Sixty-seven per cent polyepolene, thirty-eight per cent sucron, and nineteen per cent omegan,' I say, the words tripping off my tongue. 'These materials invented in a top secret laboratory, the shirts convulsive.'

My friends gasp.

'How much for one?' they ask at the same time.

'Ten dollars,' I say. 'I giving them away at ten dollars. But you can't wear them like ordinary shirts, you have to wear them in a special way. They made in England, you see, so you have to leave them hanging for two weeks before you put them on. The material have to acclimatise to the heat. After two weeks, no restrictions. I guarantee you will never see shirts like these again!'

What I fail to mention was that when I wake up, the shirt I wear to the pictures tear itself apart like it have a nightmare. It seem like sweat don't agree with it, the sun wrinkle it so that it resemble a dry trumpet bush leaf. The colours remain, but the shrivelled garment twist into something you would use for mopping your brow or wrapping up two small loaves. And that wasn't all. Ever curious, my eighteen-year old cousin Lydia who live with us, my first customer, try on her shirt straight away, so that when I return from the cinema, her baby breasts peering through two gaping holes in her chest!

But if *I* could wear new shirts, Man-Dorothy and Pancil insist, and I could see the hungry look in their eyes, if *I* have new shirt, *they* must have new shirts too. So they race home and, in less than a time, return with their ten dollars. I repeat my instructions so there would be no misunderstanding. The shirts need to hang for two weeks gentlemen, I say, the best day to start wearing them is a Sunday!

By the end of the day, having sold ten shirts at ten dollars each, I in a position to return the money I 'borrow' from my mother's purse in her handbag in the suitcase in the trunk beside her bed. And early next morning, a long queue form outside my house, I receiving visitors like a doctor offering private consultations. One at a time I give them the instructions and clinch the sale. As they depart I stress that if they open the packet before the fortnight over, the guarantee become invalid. 'Cool Fit'! people hailing me everywhere I go. The weekend newspapers proclaim the shirts 'a breath of fresh air', and Eldon Duvalle an inspiration to the young of SVG!

So, men, women and boys arriving from all over the island, everyone want a 'Cool Fit' shirt. The buyer from the department store put in an order for thirty, I turn him away with the promise of fifty 'from my next consignment'. Some come with enough money for three and four, I see the disappointment on their faces when I tell them my contract with my English suppliers forbid that.

On the evening of the following Monday a man from Rose Bank arrive when, after a long day, I taking my dinner. Bakes, and fish laced with garlic, my mother indulging me, her only son, with my favourite dish for all my hard work and enterprise. I offer the man a chunk of the fish, he wave it away with a rough sweep of the right hand. A cup of steaming cocoa? He wave that aside too, and I know I have trouble on my hands.

'The shirt melt on my back,' he grumble, taking a chair directly in front of me. 'The material thin and flaky. If this is English craftsmanship then I'm from Lima in China.'

I take a bite of the fish, add some pepper, and begin to chomp. The man staring at me while I eat, a serious look on his face. Just like some windward people can't swim, some leeward people don't joke!

'What's your name?' I ask, flicking through the book of customers I keep close to me to check details.

'Herbert Tucker,' he answer.

'Just tell me again, Herbert,' I say, 'what exactly wrong with the shirt?'

'It resemble one my brother buy from the factory at Camden

Park,' he reply, 'the only difference is that someone remove the label.'

I carry on eating while he outline his case. He curse the shirt, his bicycle, the flatness of the village, he moan about the size of the plum tree overhanging the house opposite, the smoke from next door burn his eyes, I get the impression he was a man who would grumble if the sun hot, and twice as much if it begin to rain.

'Lydia,' I call out, as he muttering away to himself, 'bring Mr Tucker a drink. He must be thirsty.'

Two minutes later Lydia push aside the net curtain and join us in the porch. She carrying a tray with bakes, fried fish, and a tall glass of mauby. With a pretty smile, she offer the tray to Herbert. He accept it, rest it on his lap and begin to eat.

'So you not happy,' I say as he chewing away, wondering what Lydia have and I don't.

'No,' he answer, 'I never see a shirt like that in my life.'

'That's because your skin not accustomed to higher fabrics like leafolene and strawricon.'

'That wasn't the fabrics you tell me,' he answer, frowning even as he eat.

'Your shirt probably build from soaperon and detolene, then. But it doesn't matter: what matter is that you wear the shirt before the atoms in the material have time to adjust to the heat and find their centre of gravity and equilibrium.'

'But since when shirts have to wear like that?' he retort. 'Since when you have to leave shirts to cure like ham? Since when you have to start wearing shirts on a Sunday as if they have magical properties?'

'So what you saying?' I ask for clarification.

'I want my money back,' he respond, biting into the last bake.

'Money back?' Now it's my turn to frown. 'Money back? Business is business, Herbert, you know that. If you buy butter from the shop and you don't like it, you can take it back? If you ride in a van and the ride bumpy and uncomfortable, you going to refuse to pay? If you sit on one buttock, you going to pay half fare?'

Herbert Tucker in his thirties, hefty, fit, but at nineteen I find that mouth-talk could keep fellas like him who moan and grumble to themselves at bay. Besides, if he look like he about to back his shirt, Lydia could always give him another pretty smile and refresh his plate. So, as he ponder, I offer a compromise.

'Tell you what, Herbert Tucker,' I say, 'as a valued customer, I going to offer you a concession.'

He finish the bakes and start on the fish. 'Go on,' he say, waiting to hear what I have in mind.

'You have children?' I ask.

'Yes. Two.'

'You married?'

'Yes.'

'When was the last time you take out the family?'

He stop eating and think about it for a while. 'Last Christmas.'

'Well, plan an outing for you and your family in a fortnight. Take them to the Botanic Gardens or Fort Charlotte. As a goodwill gesture, I'm going to give you a new shirt. And, I tell you what, since you travel such a long way, you can have one for your wife too.'

'Thanks man,' he say, perking up. 'I will make sure I treat it properly this time.'

'One thing though,' I feel I have to warn him. 'I have to ask you something: you wife chesty?'

'No,' he seem puzzled by my question. 'But she satisfy with what she have. And I don't have any complaints either.'

'Well, make sure she take an extra shirt when you go to the Gardens or the fort.'

'Why?' his puzzlement increase tenfold. 'She going to want to show off her new English shirt!'

'Just in case it cloud over,' I say, leaving it at that. 'You know how it like to rain on Sundays.'

He depart happy, and I learn from him. Whoever complain from then on, I feed them and send them home contented. If they get rowdy and raise their voice, my father come out and say 'Good Afternoon' in his gruff voice and sit on my right. If that don't work and they 'demand satisfaction', my mother materialise as if by magic. Puffing her clay pipe, the tobacco smoke drifting lazily upwards, she look them over from top to bottom to top, then order them to keep the noise down or leave her house.

When the two weeks nearly up, with over 900 dollars in the bank, my father suggest I buy a ticket to Venezuela and disappear for a couple of months. Rumour had it that Silver-hand Mack planning to boat down from Owia, he say, the family aiming to set up in the village until I refund his ten dollars. Leave right away, my father advise, come back after Christmas when the controversy die down.

There and then, sucking on her pipe, my mother contradict

him flat. Business is business, she explain to my father, *her* son issue clear instructions, she hear it with her own ears. If at their age SVG men still didn't know how to wear a shirt properly, let them take what they get!

Hungry for another exclusive, the newspapers return on the Wednesday. I cook them peas soup, Lydia make guava juice, and my mother place a bottle of rum on the table next to their bowls. After lunch and a nap, the reporter comfortable and ready to continue his work. I dress up in one of my white shirts, in the cool of the porch, I discuss the perils and joys of business. You ever see quality like that, I ask the photographer, you ever touch material so resistant and inflammatory? They take a family picture of me in my shirt, my mother brandishing her pipe, my father despondent, and Lydia grinning as though she posing for a Miss SVG contest. Then, one groggy, the other tight, they drive off at two for their next assignment in Cane Grove.

Things quieten down after the article in the papers. The fortnight over, in the week when is time to wear the shirts and I expect a flood, a mere ten customers come forward with a gripe. The final one, Hilton Prescott, was a bodybuilder from Villa, his proud black shiny muscles quivering in the heat. With a physique like that shirts wasted on him. I can't remember selling him a 'Cool Fit', but because he come all that way I accept his word.

'What kind of business you running?' he ask, refusing to take the chair I offer him.

'You have a problem?' I reply, swinging in the hammock I recently install in the porch.

'That blasted shirt you sell me,' he say, going through the action of putting on a shirt, 'before the thing get over my shoulder it come apart. I have shirts I wearing for five years without incident yet this one destroy itself the moment it come out the package. You know what would happen if I report you to the law?'

I hold up my hand to prevent him going further. 'Listen Hilton,' I say, 'what line of work you in?'

'Watchman. I'm a watchman on the Hadaway estate.'

'Then since you know how to watch things, then watch what you say,' I suggest, like my father passing on precious advice.

'How you mean?'

'Watch what you say because you talking to the law,' I warn him.

Suddenly, his mouth open, he feel the need to sit down. He ease his fourteen-stone frame onto the chair and stare at me as if he seeing a spirit. I call out to Lydia.

A few moments later Lydia stroll out with the police uniform I receive two days earlier.

'Now, what was the problem again?' I ask.

'Problem?' he say. 'Who said there was a problem?'

Lydia bring him a glass of soursop juice, he drink up, then flex his muscles.

'When you get the next consignment,' he say, as he get up to leave, 'make sure you save me one of your psychological shirts. Nineteen neck.'

feather your tingaling

With food on the table and clothes on her back, how could Melody Ambris, in the space of six months, leave a solid layer of skin from her stomach on a cocoa tree, slip from a stone in the river at Layou and sprain her left arm, and lose the piglet whose sale was to pay for her new shoes? When a teenager treats possessions as though there's an endless supply waiting to fall from the sky, what is her aunt supposed to do?

Watching the young girl a few feet away, engrossed in her simple game, bouncing a ball against a wall and catching it, Keturah Providence sat in the porch of her modest house in Retreat and wondered this. It was early evening, the sun warming down slowly, nurses, clerks and farmers trudging wearily home from their daily toil. What was she going to do with her niece, she asked herself as she chewed a tight juicy fig, was there any way she could prevent her doing some serious damage?

For Melody was an innocent. A few minutes in her company

were enough to see that. To her the world was a place of thrills, each hot day an invitation to ripe adventure. Which was fine, up to a point. But a girl like her could be dangerous: she could get hurt or, worse, she could hurt others.

Her chubby face home to smiles of every description, if she didn't meet with some terrible catastrophe, she would retain her fat, baby cheeks. Yet despite its chubbiness her face had an angelic quality. Her dark-brown eyes were large and sleepy-looking and, short like a boy's, and soft, her perfumed hair shone from the Vaseline she applied daily. Living for the delights of simple play, no one had ever seen her sad. Like a high rain cloud, her bad moods quickly passed. If she cried, it was in the privacy of her room.

Tall for fifteen, with the build of an athletic boy, Melody was undeniably feminine. Skipping everywhere, she bounced along, her sandals clicking merrily against the sole of her heel, matching the rhythm of the song she was humming or singing. For she was always with song. She fitted her name perfectly, it occurred to Keturah, or was it the other way round?

Thirty-five and childless, Keturah had jumped at the opportunity to look after Melody the afternoon her sister announced that she had found a job in Tortola. A retired American couple was interested in her, Wilma explained, the contract was to start in a fortnight. She was desperate for the post, but hadn't made arrangements for her daughter. What should she do?

Grab the opportunity, Keturah had insisted, bring Melody to live with her in Retreat. She would be a good companion, the young girl would drive out the silence and misery of the house. It was the obvious solution at the time and although she had no regrets, Keturah sometimes wondered whether she had underestimated the task of looking after a teenager.

For the Melody Keturah knew mainly through rumours and warnings from her mother quickly confirmed their truth. Easily distracted, to her time was a bother, anything that got in the way of play, a nuisance. Losing things, or losing her way, were daily occurrences. She drifted, happy in her own world, the sun on her back, a girlish joy in everything she did. A trip to the shop to buy cheese might take an hour, the cheese a squashed yellow sheet by the time she got home. On an errand for soap it wasn't unusual for her to return with a box of matches, soggy and useless. Flour for sugar, rice for bread, potatoes for biscuits, Keturah wondered how Jasmine Boucher, a distant cousin, coped with her seven children!

A handbag was the first serious loss in her new home. A brown, soft leather bag from her mother for her fifteenth birthday. Excited as only a child could be, Melody had hugged and kissed her aunt on the neck, cheeks and forehead, embarrassing Keturah with her affectionate display.

'Is perfect,' Melody screamed, as she did when excited, 'thank you mom, thank you tantie Keturah, you don't know long I pray for a bag like this!'

She caressed the bag, she smelled it, she bit it to confirm the texture. At ten that night, when Keturah went to switch off the light, Melody was cradling the bag, a picture of happiness.

September came, the seasonal rains receded, the winds cooled. Displaced for three months, the sun regained control of the sky. On the nineteenth, Keturah received an invitation to a fair in Petit Bordel. Aunt and daughter were both elated: Keturah to show off her charge and let the world know she was coping, Melody to parade her expensive birthday gift.

A handbag isn't a handbag unless it bulges and threatens to pop like a balloon! Melody had heard her mother and aunt joke about this so often, it had to be true, she felt. A handbag had to be tasteful, but it also had to be practical! If only things weren't so complicated, Melody thought, for what could she fill hers with?

Surely not the shiny pebbles from Indian Bay laid out in a circle on her dressing table, or the crumbling lizard skeletons in a saucer on the floor by the door? The half-eaten cane stalk on the kitchen table, that would do, wouldn't it?

Three exercise books and her empty geometry set were all she could find to form the base layer after an hour's search. A dibique mango, a bag of guavas, a ripe golden apple and an orange were roughly laid on these. Mustn't forget lunch. So a large plastic container was added next, leaving just enough room for the powder puff and talcum she had 'borrowed' from her aunt's bedroom. Stuffed to bursting, the bag felt right. Just after eleven, taking her aunt's hand, Melody skipped merrily to the fair.

By now, though, the precious bag had lost some of its aura. The leathery smell wasn't quite as pungent, the shine had certainly dulled. Under constant exposure to the sun the bag was beginning to shrivel like a large banana leaf. Even so her friends Carla and Clara were impressed. A handbag was sophistication, the separation of girls from giggling children. During their lunch, in the shade of a breadfruit tree, her friends took turns to stroke the bag. Like glamorous models, they practised walking with it, wriggling their hips and dipping the shoulders, heads held high and noses pointing to the sky. It was brilliant, they were forced to concede, they would give anything for one!

Melody had a hearty appetite, she was definitely a growing girl. So, for her, a snow cone topped with condensed milk was just the thing to wash down her lunch of bakes and saltfish cakes. Placing the handbag carefully on a chair where she could keep an eye on it, she crunched the snow cone and licked the milk escaping down her fingers. Simply delicious: was there anything better on a hot afternoon?

She loved to eat, she loved to play. Marbles, rounders, catch, a game could be got up anywhere. During each game she kept the bag within reach. Until, that is, a game of hopscotch, her favourite. As she chalked out the grid with her friends, she entrusted the bag to a boy with green trousers who resembled a schoolmate, Leroy Luther.

She didn't exactly *know* him, but a boy with green trousers couldn't hide, could he? Even in a crowd, she was certain he would be instantly recognisable. After watching the girls play for twenty minutes the boy passed the responsibility to a girl to eat his muffin, this girl to another as her father called time. At five, when Melody eventually located the boy in green trousers, the search began for a girl with a cream top, another with her hair in 'cane rows', and a short boy with dark glasses reading a magazine under a nutmeg tree. As the dusk closed in, Melody was forced to admit that the bag was well and truly lost.

On her way home, empty-handed, deflated, she wished she wasn't so trusting. The first boy had promised to look after the bag, yet he had gone and lost it! She would never trust a boy again, she vowed. Head down, she trudged wearily from Petit Bordel to Retreat, rehearsing the song to sing to her aunt. For she had a song for everything. Wilma had warned her about this, so Keturah had grown to respond with a verse of her own. As soon as she entered the house Melody began:

> *Me lost, me lost*
> *The leather handbag*
> *Me take it to the fair*
> *But a thief did a sprag*

And Keturah replied immediately:

> *Girl go look under a stone*
> *Girl go search breadfruit tree*
> *Girl go retrace your step*
> *Just bring the bag home to me.*

After the handbag, a piglet. A cute, jet-black six-week old given to running around in circles, to which Melody had grown quite attached. The piglet was one of seven. Melody would sit for hours watching them suckle or jostling to be first to get at their feed. In their haste they fell over themselves, squealing and grunting with each accident. She liked their mindlessness, they were like helpless children.

Whenever he visited Keturah, Crisco Magro, her boyfriend, would stare at the sow and its young ones, nod several times, and grin. Was he as captivated by their behaviour as she was? Melody wondered. But where Melody saw a source of wonder, where Keturah saw an investment to provide food and clothes,

Crisco saw the dowry for their wedding.

'Feed the pigs good, you know,' he would command Melody, 'make sure they get the youngest bananas and the finest wee-wee-wee.'

'We running out of bananas,' Melody told him one Sunday.

'No problem,' Crisco answered, 'I will load some in the car tomorrow.'

'The wee-wee-wee going down too,' Melody added, 'only two bundles left.'

'Relax, my little dumpling,' said Crisco, 'another juicy bundle coming Wednesday.'

They waited a week, a fortnight, a month, nothing. The care of the animals was left to Melody and Keturah. Fetching bags of wee-wee-wee from the mountains, dragging green bananas up the hill to the kitchen, feeding the animals and clearing away the mess, they worked tirelessly while Crisco looked on, repeating his promises to help but reluctant to get his hands dirty.

Melody adored the little piglets as much as she detested Crisco. To her he was coarse and vulgar. Tall and thin, with a narrow face, his big eyes bulged scarily. He drank heavily and, when he won at cards, he celebrated with cheap cigarettes. His shirts were all too short, his trousers sat low on his hips revealing his hairy lower back. When reminded of his promises he would shrug his shoulders and scowl, 'I bringing them tomorrow: what happen, little *tingalingaling*, you can't wait?'

There was something else about him that made Melody uneasy. Did she imagine it, she often wondered, or did it actually occur? One evening, after a hard day counting out thousands of dollars at the bank, Keturah had crashed out on the settee.

Melody was cutting out pictures of her favourite cricketers from a magazine and Crisco was reading the newspaper.

'Get me a red-belly tart,' Keturah had commanded. 'And a cup of black coffee! Those flipping customers at the bank: they will be the death of me!'

Concentrating hard on her task, Melody didn't hear her aunt's request. Crisco coughed and looked in Melody's direction. No response. He coughed several times. Still no response from Melody.

'What happen, Melody?' he growled. 'You deaf or something? Go and fetch your aunt the red-belly and coffee!'

Melody was wearing green shorts beneath a white shirt. On the way to the kitchen she was sure she could feel Crisco's eyes on her. From that time, the moment he pulled up in his old car, his 'taxi', whose only passenger had been a teenager rushed to hospital to give birth, the instant Melody heard the clanging and rattling, she would race to her room or excuse herself and go outside to play with her friends.

She fed the piglets every night. Their diet was green bananas boiled until they were soft enough for their young, tender snouts. Small and frail, they ate, fought and slept in an untidy heap in the pen in the yard by the kitchen. Dependent on her for their food, she loved it when they tickled her fingers with their warm snouts. When they fed the animals together at weekends, she could sense her aunt's dilemma: there wasn't enough space to rear the brood, and feeding all eight took a large share of her wages. Costly now, Melody was aware, as the pigs got older, it would be an even greater struggle to feed them.

One morning, needing new shoes for school, Keturah directed Melanie to take one of the piglets to Mr Fraser at the other end of the village. In return she was to collect two hundred dollars. It was to be a day to forget.

It wasn't a long journey. Divided into three distinct regions, High-village, Low-village and 'No-go' village, an area where children were forbidden because its inhabitants gambled, smoked and cursed until they were broke, on a cool morning a walk round Retreat cost a fit adult fifteen minutes, a forgetful child, thirty. So it was a short trip. Along the narrow concrete road until this gave way to a mud track, a left turn at Mrs Springer's house with its plumrose tree pregnant with pink fruits. A shortcut through Mr Minetta's yard where the wooden kitchen was almost the same size as the house, and you were there.

A few minutes into the journey the piglet began to wriggle. It grunted and squealed as though it was being murdered, it twisted and wriggled like a baby with severe wind. Melody felt sorry for it. Its narrow tiny eyes looked sad and frightened. She wished she could keep it and care for it. Heaven knew what Mr Fraser was going to do with the poor wretch! Perhaps rear it, then sell it on, a year later, at a handsome profit. Whatever it was, she couldn't bear the thought of being separated from the piglet.

At the plum tree in Mrs Roach's yard, she stopped. But for an occasional snort, the piglet had now calmed. Melody lowered herself onto the grass then, when she was comfortable, she placed the piglet on her lap. She stroked its back gently and offered it a finger to nibble.

'I will come and see you,' she reassured it, 'the bananas and sweet vine you like, I will bring you plenty.'

As though it understood her, the piglet stopped trembling and sat quietly on her lap.

'You like plums,' Melody asked it, 'pigs eat plums?'

The piglet grunted. Directly above her head Melody pointed to a ripe bunch. Yellow and aromatic, she loved them, and she was sure the piglet would too.

'Stay here,' she said to the piglet, 'I'm going to pick some plums.'

She placed the piglet on the grass, stroked its back and begged it, 'Don't move, you know.'

When she was satisfied that the piglet was comfortable she mounted the tree and was soon in its heart .

'Ten, eleven, twelve,' she called down, after a couple of minutes, 'fifteen plums should enough, not true, piglet? Don't move, you know, don't forget what I tell you.'

A few minutes later Melody descended. She formed two piles of plums, the soft yellow ones for the piglet, and the half-ripe plums for herself. Only as she turned to offer the piglet its share did she realise that it had gone. She felt sick. Her belly began to ache, her head began to swell. Warm tears filled her eyes.

She searched under the tree, she thrashed the long grass with a stick.

'Piglet,' Melody called out, softly at first, 'where are you?'

She climbed the tree again to get a better view of the land. She scoured the area leading to the mountains, the main road back to the village, and the arrowroot field to her left.

'Piglet, come back, please, or my aunt will kill me.'

Two hours later, she knew she would have to compose another song for her aunt.

Before Melody moved in, Crisco visited Keturah three times a week. He liked to hear of the huge sums deposited by customers at the bank, loved to touch the fingers that had been in contact with bundles of crisp notes. With the arrival of the piglets he was round every day.

'Beautiful little animals, eh, Keturah,' he said one Monday night, 'when they older we can sell three of the pigs and buy goats.'

'You have a buyer in mind?' Keturah asked, for she had been thinking the same thing.

'No, but pigs always in demand.'

'How much you think one would go for?'

'Five hundred dollars: more if you sell to the right person.'

'That's a good price.'

'And that's just the start,' Cisco confided, as though the animals were his. 'We can sell the goats and buy cows: a healthy cow can fetch 3000 dollars, you know. Then we can sell some of the cows and buy a plot of land.'

'How come you know so much about animals?' Keturah asked, for although she had seen him watching the pigs feed, she couldn't remember him showing them any affection.

'I grow up with pigs and dogs,' Crisco replied.

'And the prices: you sure you get them right?'

'A man in my position have to know the price of everything.'

'So you know the price of a wedding, then?' Keturah asked. 'And you know what your share be?'

'Share, Keturah, share?' Crisco seemed confused. 'What you talking about?'

'I bringing half to the wedding, Crisco, so you have to bring half too.'

'I bringing my car,' Crisco sat back and crossed his legs.

'Your *car*?' Keturah couldn't hide her contempt. 'The sow

alone worth more than that old jalopy! '

'Jalopy?' Crisco fumed, 'you calling my motor a jalopy?'

'What it is, then?'

'Next time you want a driving lesson, when you want to go for a Sunday drive, you will find out!'

Grabbing his worn sandals, he had stormed off into the night. For three days he had stayed away. Now, though, the money from the sale of the piglet due, he was waiting with Keturah when Melody returned.

Melody sang:

> *Me lost, me lost*
> *The little piglet*
> *Me place it under a tree*
> *To get a little rest*

And Keturah answered:

> *Girl go back to the tree*
> *Girl go look carefully*
> *Two hundred dollars or else*
> *A woman left on the shelf*

She had lost her birthday present, a full scale search with her friends the following day didn't produce the piglet. Two hundred dollars gone, just like that. Stoic, fantastic, Keturah tried hard to understand. She didn't curse, she didn't get angry. In time, Melody would grow up, she felt sure, one day she would learn. Like mothers, aunts had to accept disappointment, she told herself, it was part of their job.

And for the next two months, apart from spraining her left

hand, there was little to complain about. Each shopping trip ended with the correct change, she did her homework before meeting her friends. Keturah watched Melody playing in the road, at marbles, cricket or rounders, and saw a calmer girl now, less abrasive, settled. There were no tantrums, no tossing the ball away in frustration and having to retrieve it. She was definitely growing up.

Observing and assessing the animals as they increased in weight and size, Crisco now visited twice a day. Soon they'd be ready, he advised Keturah. Beautiful animals, healthy and alert, each worth at least 500 dollars, they were nearly there, Keturah agreed, 'they were coming to come'. The plans could go ahead.

'I going to trade in the old car,' Crisco promised Keturah one Sunday after a delicious lunch of rice and stewed pork. 'I cut back on rum and cigarettes, I ready when you ready.'

Keturah set the date for the wedding and preparations began.

A bridesmaid! She was going to be a bridesmaid! Melody couldn't sleep the night Keturah made the announcement. She accompanied her aunt to Kingstown to choose the material for their dresses, she invited Carla and Clara the moment they returned. She began to save for a new handbag.

The Sunday before the wedding, Keturah and her friends cleaned the house from top to bottom and swept the yard. There were new pillows, new cushions, the bats that hid in the roof were driven out. The sow and the remaining pigs were moved to her father's yard.

Melody's job that Sunday was to wash, dry and iron the tablecloth, and to clean and polish the dining table to the standard the women had set. What wasn't new had to be shiny clean. Mesmerised by the preparations, and given to procrastination, she spent the morning watching the others work instead of getting on with her task.

'Melody,' Keturah warned several times, 'get yourself down to the river!'

'I'm going,' Melody would reply, 'just getting ready.'

An hour later, still dreaming of the big day, when Keturah called out, 'Melody!' it was the same answer.

In the middle of the afternoon, as she contemplated the task before her, she heard the spluttering of Crisco's car. In one swift motion she yanked the tablecloth from the table and dumped it into a large basket. Off to the river she sped to complete her chore. But in her haste she had gathered not just the cloth but the knives, forks, cups and spoons Keturah had laid out on the table. As she opened the tablecloth, with a mocking metallic song, the contents slipped into the swiftly flowing river, cutlery, rice, sugar, milk and flour disappearing before her eyes.

Melody was aghast. She froze. Snatching frantically at the water, gathering frothy fistfuls, she screamed in horror.

'No!' she cried. 'Come back knife, come back fork, come back spoon and flour!'

She watched as the current swept them away to the sea nearby. What was she going to tell her aunt? Where would she find the words? All the way home she thought of how to break the news. She had ruined Keturah's plans, what she got she deserved.

An exhausted Keturah was resting on a wooden stool in the porch when she returned and, a cigarette at the corner of his mouth, Crisco was polishing the car. She couldn't say it so Melody sang, in a faltering voice, tears streaming down her face:

Me lost, me lost
The tablecloth
Me take it to the river
Full up of rice and flour

Horrified, the words tottering from her mouth, her left hand covering her eyes in exasperation, Keturah responded:

Not just rice and flour
What about spoon and knife?
So thanks to you and Jennings river
I will never be a wife.

Melody began to sob. She cried, she wailed, her face was covered in fresh tears. Her aunt's treasured cutlery set from England was at the bottom of the river and all because of her! She started for her room.

'Wait,' Crisco shouted, 'you stay right there!'

Melody froze on the spot. She turned slowly and lowered her head in shame. Keturah dragged herself up from the stool and held out her arms.

'Come,' she said, 'come Melody, come. What is gone is gone.'

But Crisco was furious. His eyes bulged as though they might pop from their sockets. Copying Keturah, he began to sing to Melody:

You lose handbag and pig
You singe your aunt new wig
Your aunt finger want ring
But you give river everything

So girl go feather your tingalingaling
Girl go feather your tingalingaling
Girl go feather your tingalingaling
Girl go feather your tingalingaling

Keturah stood there, mouth open, in disbelief. She was shocked that Crisco had burst into song, but his suggestion?

'Out,' Keturah ordered him. 'Get out of my house!'

'Why,' Crisco affected innocence, 'what did I do?'

'What kind of suggestion you making to a young girl like Melody?'

'Young girl: Melody isn't a young girl, she old enough to understand.'

'Get out,' Keturah yelled, 'get your nasty self out of my house before I have to throw you out!'

As Crisco shuffled out, Keturah went over and hugged Melody.

'Ignore him,' she said, 'he won't be back here, I promise you.'

'What was he singing about?' Melody asked.

'Forget that,' said Keturah, 'thanks for saving me from a man like that.'

late

'Susan, go and call your sister, tell her dinner's ready.'

'Helen isn't home yet, Mother.'

'What? But it's after seven o'clock!'

'Seven o'clock, eight, when was the last time Helen was home before dark?'

'The three of us had dinner on Tuesday, didn't we? Or was it Monday?'

'Mother, Helen has been late every single day for the last three weeks, stop burying your head in the sand.'

'But college finishes at four. What calling a young girl like her have coming home when people closing up their house for the night?'

'It's your fault and you know it, mother. I told you to warn her in February but you said to give her time to settle into the Community College. This is an eighteen-year old who's been travelling to the High School in Kingstown since she was twelve! Come on, Mother, *you* know, *I* know, everybody knows the reason why Helen doesn't get home till it's dark.'

'Susan, I don't know: I honestly don't know.'

'You mean you don't *want* to.'

'I've never been a woman to listen to rumours.'

'Then it's time to start. You must be the only one who doesn't see her climbing out of Cleeve Neptune's car and waving goodbye to him as if she is a big woman.'

'Cleeve Neptune is a respectable man, I don't like what you insinuating.'

'Cleeve? Respectable? Mother, open your eyes and see what the whole village can't help but notice. Take the wool out your ears and hear what people are saying about Helen and her fancy man.'

'You mustn't say bad things about people, Susan, that's not how your father and I brought you up. If you don't have evidence, keep your mouth shut. If you do, keep it to yourself or in the family: leave newsmongering to those who have nothing better to do with their time.'

'Mother, listen, Cleeve isn't the man you think he is, believe me.'

'Cleeve is a decent man.'

'If you knew him properly you wouldn't say that.'

'I know all I need to know. I see him in church every Sunday with his family. He is the first one there, he doesn't miss a service. Rain, storm, even the threat of hurricane can't prevent him attending.'

'Going to church doesn't prove anything.'

'You have no right to talk like that, Susan! You're young, you don't know about these matters. You disparaging a man who makes the effort to dress up in shirt and tie every Sunday God brings, a man who drives miles in the scorching heat with his family to be amongst people who believe! And you want me to doubt his character?'

'I'm not asking you to do anything, mother. *I* know Cleeve, *everyone* knows Cleeve.'

Susan Wiley and her mother, Anetta, lived in Gordon Village on the leeward side of SVG. Two miles from the calm sea at Lashum, Gordon Village is lush and mountainous. With a permanent cover of mist, it gives the impression of being further in the interior than it actually is. A narrow, pitched road describes a rough oval shape through the village, with even narrower tributaries to Coco, Jack Hill, Mangaroo and Barree. Bananas, dasheen, carrots, yams, coconut, tannias, onions and oranges grow everywhere, the land is fertile to the point where guava seeds carelessly tossed onto a grassy bank sprout with the first droplets of rain.

Like its neighbours, Gordon Village is tiny and easy to miss by those who cling to the coastal road, knowing the mainland superficially like tourists in a haste to taste everything but chew nothing. But, like villages everywhere, it has a personality of its own. There are over a hundred families related by blood, obligation, or blind loyalty, newcomers quickly assume the Gordon drawl. A sense of community pervades most things, it is all for one or not at all.

By the time she was fifty, Anetta Wiley, a midwife, had had hundreds of deliveries to her credit. Now, five years later, her professionalism and reputation assured, the trust she had built in the district matched the confidence she had in Cleeve Neptune.

'Cleeve is a stalwart in the church,' she repeated to her doubting daughter. 'I would trust him with you, and I trust him with Helen, no matter how late he delivers her home.'

'So you haven't heard the rumours then?' Susan retorted, in the weary tone of one who doesn't want to prolong a conversation but feels obliged to say what needs to be said.

'I told you, I don't listen to rumours.'

'Not even when they involve a fifty-year old married man taking home students?'

'Where is the harm in that? Since when an adult can't give a child a lift home in SVG? This is the Caribbean, Susan, not England or America where depraved people snatch children and commit all manner of evil!'

'He only gives lifts to girls, mother, that's where the problem is. You never see a boy in his car, not a single one. Sixteen, seventeen, eighteen: Cleeve doesn't care how old the passengers are: so long as they are girls.'

'I don't believe you, Susan, I can't believe you. Cleeve Neptune is from a respectable family. They own acres of land, they long-established in this blessed country of ours. They run a shoe-shop in Kingstown, they import goods from Trinidad. Those sardines you like, the condensed milk and tinned fruits in the kitchen cupboard, they're the people you have to thank. Cleeve is a mechanic, a farmer and a businessman. One of his sisters is a lawyer and so is his wife. And you want me to believe that such a man would harm a daughter of mine?'

'You might think you are Cleeve's friend, but do you believe Cleeve sees you as *his* friend?'

'He's a Christian, and I have faith in those who commit themselves to Christ.'

'You can swear for him?'

'I don't swear, Susan. And even if I did, I wouldn't swear for anyone.'

'So you wouldn't swear for me?'

'You are my daughter, Susan, I trust you and pray that no harm befall you: but I don't know where you are every hour of the day, do I? Parents have to believe what children tell them, for without trust, where would the world be?'

'And it's the same with Cleeve, is it? You are putting me in the same category as a man with his reputation?'

'It's not for me to judge, I told you.'

'Mother, you are amazing.'

'Even if Cleeve was that way inclined, why would he bother with schoolgirls when, with his money, he could have older, more mature women for *company*?'

Susan turned to her right and stared disbelievingly at her mother sitting on a wooden stool beside her. Fifty-five, with a small, delicate circular mouth, her mother could pass as their elder sister, it occurred to her. Streaks of grey, dense at the temples, couldn't detract from the calm beauty of her face. She was like a sister, she could be frustratingly unworldly at times.

'Mother, you might be a midwife,' Susan said, 'but sometimes you act so naïve. You carry on like someone who actually believes that babies fall from the sky.'

How much her mother knew, Susan could only guess. Her

head constantly buried in some medical book, Anetta Wiley lived for her children and her work. In training and practice, she hadn't lost a single baby, and she had no intention of relinquishing that record. But it was impossible for her not to have an inkling, Susan was convinced, someone in the district must have taken her aside and had a quiet word. Villages thrive on gossip, Susan knew from bitter experience, those confined to bed might not hear directly, or in the first wave, but rumours have a way of finding their way to any waiting door. If her mother didn't know, it was a case of not wishing to know.

A businessman with a reputation for driving a hard bargain, those who witnessed Cleeve dropping off his passengers were convinced he extracted his fare in other ways. Charity doesn't make for good business, and no one had ever accused him of being a Good Samaritan. Men like him, with money and influence, fed and bought drinks casually, but there were always ulterior motives. There'd be a favour to call in at some later date, a rival to scare off, or a guard dog to poison. So he attracted an army of followers who liked the idea of being linked to a man known for his generosity, but most of all, he was attractive to young, impressionable girls.

Cleeve had no shame, the men of the village would say as he disgorged his daily passenger, what a pity Helen's father was abroad. Someone needed to stand up to him. He had to be challenged, to do nothing was to let him get away with blue murder. But no champion ever came forward. No one had the courage to say to his face what they whispered behind his back.

'He lucky Helen isn't my daughter,' old Crosby Brown said to his companion, Dylan Henry, as they watched Cleeve's Land

Rover pull up one evening. 'He lucky I not closely related to the Wileys, or he would pay dearly for his immoral ways!'

'You fool,' Dylan stuttered, recognising the futility of the threat, 'is none of our business. The country have laws to protect the vulnerable. Besides, Helen isn't a child, she old enough to know her own mind.'

But Crosby wanted retribution. He cursed Helen on her way to college, at every sighting he whispered names that would have embarrassed or crushed others. Her reaction was always the same. She looked him in the eye, turned up her nose, then walked slowly away. Whispers and scandal didn't bother her. Where another girl would have slipped silently out of the car and melted swiftly into the darkness, Helen didn't mind advertising her arrival.

Lingering by the car, in full view of those who welcomed the early evening at the roadside exchanging stories about the day, she would stroke Cleeve's hairy arm and play with his stout fingers. Clasping her expensive leather handbag in her left hand, she would turn and wave provocatively on the walk to her home.

'Dylan, see all the style that girl have,' Crosby sneered one Tuesday as they watched her strolling home, 'her house sure to burn down one day.'

'Leave the girl alone,' Dylan recommended, 'she young, let her flap her wings. She'll come down from the sky when she ready.'

'She can't: once a young girl taste high life is impossible to rein her back in.'

'You think so?'

'I know so.'

'Well, I don't agree.'

'That's because you don't know anything about the world of men and women. But I tell you, and mark my words, Dylan Henry, Helen can't stop herself and she won't. I just pray that she doesn't end up with style alone like so many young girls nowadays. Because Helen have *too much* style.'

'How a person can have too much style?'

'Because it's not real style, is just something she see and imitate. Somebody will break her leg: and then we'll see where style can get her.'

It was the casual way they talked, the old men and boys, the girls and women of the village, protective yet willing to offer up the sacrifice. Incensed by her indifference to rumours and accusations, affronted by the way she turned up her nose at them as though they stank, at their bitterest they wished to see her fall. Yet, in private, they couldn't help but admire the way she lived. Defiant, wanting for nothing, seemingly above their gossip and whispers, they begrudged her lifestyle as much as they loathed her.

The men and boys couldn't compete with Cleeve. Money and infamy were too great an advantage to overhaul. He was bound to win, they conceded, it would take a brave man to stop him, or some crazed woman who had given him her all and had nothing further to lose. Helen was doomed, the elders could sense. But she was too young to perceive the signs, or to care.

Building on the legacy of his bed-ridden mother, Cleeve was a prodigious traveller on the family's behalf. He knew the leeward coast of the mainland as intimately as the windward, Bequia and Union were just a brief plane-ride away. In order to finalise a deal he might stay overnight, if he had drunk too much to celebrate, some distant relative or 'friend' would materialise with the offer of a bed, and 'breakfast' the following morning. He was comfortable with this life of travelling and fresh beds, 'hospitality' he took in his stride.

A hard-drinking businessman, he made friends easily. Enemies were eventually charmed. Those who remained outside his reach still deserved a drink if they didn't object.

On the return from his travels, Helen would be there at the airport or harbour with a welcoming grin, a child-lover, her studies abandoned, another forged absent note in her bag to deflect inquisitive teachers. Light-headed after an afternoon together, in the evening, she would drive the twenty miles home, aching for her bed, but too intoxicated to sleep. Early or late, as she sighed sweetly in her dreams, Cleeve would pull up at the nearest shop for 'a final brandy'. A rum for those men who refrained from judging him, a cold malt for the women, and it might be midnight before he returned to his family in Sandy Bay.

Cleeve's girl, despised, envied or admired, Helen had no time for friends. Tall, heavily-built, devastatingly ordinary in looks, he was her everything. The crushing ordinariness of his wide, lumpy face was rescued by a bushy beard. Solid in face, fond of food and drink, his stomach was large and round. Helen loved its shape and volume: it was a part of what he symbolised, fullness, plenty, he was the essence of a 'big man'.

In daylight his skin was yellowish-black, at night, a dull bronze. His hair, a black mass, resembled an uncurled afro. She loved his colour, his hair, his extravagance, his suffocating hug. The aura of money and notoriety compensating for his lack of pretension, she committed herself totally to him.

She loved him. In her mind she was certain of that. She loved him, and he loved her. He had taught her to drive, he paid for her textbooks, he provided whatever she desired. When he was too tired to perform he would sit up in bed and she would dance for him. Her black slender body a sinuous wave, her girlish grin setting off the charge in him, brandy and Helen were a lethal cocktail. She loved him, his wishes were her command, her wishes and indulgencies, his.

With land and inheritance, money had never been an obstacle for him. He chose her dresses, he reimbursed her impulsive purchases of shoes and skirts. When she argued for the tights popular with women of 'superior status', he gave in without fuss.

In Cleeve, in a world for two, she had everything she craved. Others could wait for tomorrow, she was having her milk and honey today. Cleeve might disappear for a month on business, or tied up with work, could only manage an occasional phone call. Knowing that the absences were temporary, she could put up with them. Her monthly allowance of three hundred dollars was secure, there'd be a new dress, perfume, and shoes to make up for his absence. In Cleeve, doomed as he was, she had all she wished for.

'Finished your dinner already, Susan?'

'Yes mother, I was really hungry. There was a problem with the computers at work today so we had to work through lunch. At least they let us leave early.'

'You didn't have anything to eat?'

'Just a tulum that was at the bottom of my bag, and a glass of water.'

'You should wake up early and cook your lunch to take to work: that's what I used to do when I was training to be a midwife in Kingstown.'

'That was then, mother: nowadays when you have a hundred places to eat in town at a decent price, only a fool would carry lunch.'

They talked like this for a few minutes, comparing prices at the restaurants and the quality of the food, then Mrs Wiley pulled her chair closer to her daughter.

'Susan, I have something to tell you,' she whispered.

'Yes mother?' Susan said, mildly curious.

'Helen's late,' she said in a hushed voice, as though she feared being overheard.

'No she isn't, mother,' Susan replied. 'She's probably in her room. I saw her going for a shower twenty minutes ago.'

'I know she's home: I didn't mean late from college, I mean *late* late.'

'Oh my God!'

Susan sat up in the chair and looked her mother directly in the eye.

'Yes. That's what she's gone and done,' Mrs Wiley closed her eyes as if to shut out the world.

'How late, mother? Did she say?'

'Three weeks.'

'That damn girl, that stupid fool, I thought she had more sense than that. No wonder she's been spending so much time locked up in the bathroom.'

' Susan, I'm sorry, I should have listened to you.'

'Listen to me, mother? Since when do you listen to me? I warned you, but what did you say? Cleeve is a gentleman, Helen is too sensible to get into trouble!'

'Susan, please, I can't take it, I can't understand it. How am I going to tell her father? What will the people in the church say?'

'The church people can say what they please, good luck when you tell dad.'

'Just look at what that girl has got herself into,' Mrs Wiley shook her head, disbelievingly, 'a scholarship student, intelligent, and this is all she will have to show for those years studying.'

'Where's the baby going to live?' Susan asked.

'Right here, Susan, where else? I can't put her out.'

'It's another mouth to feed.'

'We're Caribbean people, Susan: you make a child, you bring the child! You have to find a way to clothe and feed it.'

'The house is small, mother.'

'When the baby's old enough she will have to find her own place.'

'Where is she, mother, where is the arrogant little madam?'

'No matter what she's done, Susan, she's still your sister, don't talk like that.'

'Just tell her to come out here!'

Mrs Wiley got up from the table, heavily, for a woman of her slight stature, and climbed the stairs to the bedroom. Five minutes later, as Susan sat at the kitchen table trying to make sense of what she had just heard, her mother returned. Her hunched shoulders told of the outcome of the exchange.

Within the house Helen had created a home of her own. The

furnishings in her bedroom made the rest of the house appear bare and inadequate. Her dressing table was a dark mahogany, two small adjustable side mirrors complementing the large central one. Three luxurious wooden chairs supplemented the stool at the dressing table, on top of which stood five expensive bottles of perfume and two dainty tubs of hand cream.

Three enormous framed photographs of herself, one at the airport in Barbados, the second in Palm Island, and the last at her graduation, filled the wall opposite the bed. A gold watch in its case, and a silver portable radio, stood on the bedside table. Half-open, bulging under the weight of dresses and shoes, a wooden wardrobe stood to the left of the bed. An aroma of perfume and body lotion pervaded the room and, as Susan and her mother entered, it occurred to her that her younger sister had probably sprayed the perfume to welcome them, before racing back to bed.

'Congratulations, Helen,' Susan said, sarcastically, taking a chair at the same time as her mother, 'well done.'

Lying in bed, a white bed sheet up to her neck as though there were mosquitoes to keep out, Helen didn't take the bait.

'What's the matter,' Susan continued in the same sarcastic tone, 'don't you want to celebrate the happy event?'

'Leave her alone,' Mrs Wiley intervened, 'don't be too hard on her.'

'Leave her alone, mother, leave her alone? What next, you're going to say she's just a child?'

'She is, Susan, Helen is just a child. She might be eighteen but when you think about it seriously, she is still a girl.'

'I'm not a child,' Helen spoke for the first time, slowly,

carefully, and in a surprisingly calm voice, 'and I can talk for myself, thank you.'

'See, mother,' said Susan, 'and there you were thinking she was all innocent coming home at midnight! When she ran off last Wednesday evening claiming she was going to revise for her exams with her friends, you swallowed that like a giant kingfish. Well, she's got what she was looking for, hasn't she? And when her pretty bundle arrives she will end up like all the other girls who carry their sense between their legs.'

'Don't call my child a bundle!' Helen said in the same composed voice. 'My child will have a mother and a father, thank you.'

'Father? What father?' Susan asked, matching her sister's calm tone. 'Where will it get a father from?'

'Cleeve, that's where!'

'Cleeve is going to mind the baby, is he?'

'Cleeve looks after his children!'

'His children with his wife, you mean. What about the others he has scattered about the place?'

'Cleeve doesn't have "outside" children: all the things people say about him are not true. They're just lies, cruel lies!'

'So you've given him the good news, then? You've told him about your little joy?'

'Of course I've told him: he's the father, isn't he?'

'And he was happy, I take it: he took you out to dinner for a little celebration?'

'He's going to marry me.'

'Marry you? Helen, are you dotish or something?'

'As soon as he divorces his wife, we're going to get married.'

Mrs Wiley began to sob. Pitiful, snivelling, pathetic whimpers, her head buried in her hands. Her own mother had had faith in her while she trained for her vocation and similarly, she had passed on to her daughters the freedom she enjoyed. And now this! Privileged, clever, Helen had now descended to the level of the dozens of young girls she saw weekly at the hospital.

Still sobbing, tears streaming down her cheeks, she got up, left the room and headed downstairs, wondering where she had failed. As though by mutual agreement, the sisters waited until she had safely cleared the bottom stair before resuming.

'Cleeve and his wife don't get on,' Helen explained now that Mrs Wiley had gone, 'they sleep in separate rooms, they haven't had sex for two years. She doesn't turn him on, he doesn't find her attractive. The next time she goes away on holiday to Canada, that's it, he says, they're finished, marriage over.'

'And you believe that story? You believe Cleeve is going to leave his wife and children for a schoolgirl? Do you honestly think he's going to destroy his businesses for you?'

'Cleeve loves me, Susan, and I love him.'

'What do you know about love?'

'I know more than you, and I'll have a baby to prove it.'

'You fool, you stupid girl: listen to me: Cleeve has girls all over the place: he's not going to leave his wife: the moment he finds out you're pregnant he'll find another girl to replace you.'

'Like the way I replaced you, Susan?' Diane said with a wicked chuckle.

'What did you say?' Susan asked, sweat appearing under her armpits.

'You call me stupid, but you are the one who will look

foolish,' Susan answered with relish.

Helen removed the sheet and sat up in the bed.

'Just wait till I tell mother,' she continued. 'Just wait till I tell her that you used to go with Cleeve when you started working at the bank. You thought I didn't know, didn't you? But I know everything, Cleeve told me. I know all your secrets, you self-righteous bitch.

'Your little secret places, how many dresses he bought you, I bet you didn't realise he kept a record, right down to the price he paid! I know everything, every minute detail! He even showed me the way you nibble when you kiss. I know everything, Susan, down to what you were like in bed! He told me, he showed me how you move. Only, he says I'm ten times better than you.

'*I'm* not the one that's stupid, *you* are: *I'll* have something to show the world that me and Cleeve were lovers, and what do *you* have? Nothing. That's the difference between us, Susan. He had to bring me straight to my door, I made him. I wouldn't let him drop me off at the main road. I didn't sneak about like a thief in the night!'

'You win, Helen,' Susan could barely say the words, so shocked was she at her sister's revelation, 'you win, but you're making a big mistake. Cleeve didn't finish with me, I finished with him.'

'Oh yeah?'

'Yes, I was the one who ended it. I was fed up of his bad ways and his smoking and drinking. I couldn't take his money, I didn't like the way he believed he could buy me. I wanted to pay my own way. That cashier's job where I started out: I worked hard to get it, no one pulled strings for me. I left him because I saw sense,

I got out despite all his grand promises. I was twenty-two then, I made a terrible mistake getting involved with his kind. Fortunately, I quickly discovered he wasn't worth it. And if he told you you're ten times better than me in bed, then good for you. And good for him!'

'I know you think Cleeve only wants me for sex, but he's not like that. He loves me, he respects me. It's not just bedroom business with us. He admires me, he can just sit there and watch me dance or fool around. We're together, I tell you. We're in love!'

'You childish, naïve, foolish imbecile,' Susan said, the extent of the delusion now apparent, 'you're willing to slash your own throat? Just look at you, trying to act like a woman when you're just a pathetic teenager. You're wasting your life, Helen! You're trading in your ambitions for someone like Cleeve! Look how that man have you!

'You used to be so bright, you used to come top in Chemistry and Physics, and now you sound like one of those country girls who never completed a full day in school! And all because of a fifty-year old man who dangle his money in front your eyes! But don't you worry, Cleeve will come to Gordon Village one night: he'll discover how dark the night in SVG can be!'

Farmer, mechanic, builder, Cleeve Neptune also rented apartments in Villa. Compact, with a sumptuous view of Bequia, and a mile from the airport at Arnos Vale, the four apartments were in constant demand. He owned a fifth, but this was private. He used it for business, and it served as a home when he was too tired or drunk to negotiate the treacherous windward roads at night.

For twelve days Susan watched for his car outside the

apartment. Directly after work in Kingstown, she caught a van to Arnos Vale, got off at the Shell petrol station and walked the quarter of a mile to the bus stop from which she could observe the building. Twelve days, nothing. She went for long walks to Calliaqua, read even the sports section of the newspapers, waved away country vans in search of a fare. She waited. Familiar with Cleeve's lifestyle, and having glimpsed his vehicle in town, she knew he wasn't abroad. Patience, she told herself, be patient, he was in the country, he would eventually turn up. He had to.

On the thirteenth evening, she saw the Honda turn right at the corner at the base of the hill. It pulled up on the right hand side of the road. She made out the huge figure wrestling his way out of the car. Now that the moment had arrived, her heart thudded against the walls of her chest. Her stomach churned, she felt sick. The tingling of panic spread throughout her body. She no longer wished to meet him.

But to get this far and withdraw quietly? She would never forgive herself. Her old age would be spent cursing the coward in her. At 9.13pm every Thursday, she would be haunted by the memory of this night. Hot and sweaty, daring and nerves in a bitter contest, she begged for courage, pleaded with her body not to betray her.

Skipping across the road, she scampered the two hundred metres to the apartment and rapped five times like someone desperate to escape a heavy downpour. The ten-second wait seemed an eternity. Then he was there. Shirt unbuttoned, staring at her from a great height, he sported an enormous grin like a parent welcoming home a wayward child after a long absence. Susan pushed past him into the apartment.

It hadn't changed since her last visit three years earlier. It still doubled effortlessly as an office and a home. The front door led to a narrow corridor, at the end of which was the living room. A brown leather settee backed onto the wall on the left as she entered, a television set and DVD player, their connecting wires entangled, stood proudly by the solitary window. A side door opened to the kitchen and well-stocked bar. On a large purpose-built table in the centre of the room stood an idle computer, and a bottle of whisky next to it told Susan that Cleeve still had the old habit.

'Susan!' Cleeve said as she stood there feeling anxious and trying to quell the doubts about the wisdom of her visit, 'what you doing here girl?'

'I came to see you.'

'Well sit down nuh, girl, what you doing standing there like a stranger?'

'Thanks.'

Susan eased herself onto the settee and placed her handbag on the floor next to her. The memories came flooding back. Of three months of long evenings, of the excuses she fabricated to explain getting home late. She heard a clink, the aroma of the whisky reached her, and before she knew, Cleeve was standing over her, a tall glass with ice in one hand and a malt in the other.

'Here you are, Susan,' Cleeve said, in the tone of a man at ease with women, 'a whisky for me and a malt for you.'

'Thanks,' Susan said, 'you have a good memory.'

'How could I forget a girl like you?'

'You've forgotten many girls, Cleeve, we both know that.'

'And many girls have forgotten me.'

'But you would be in credit, of course.'

'Naturally. I'm a businessman, after all. What's the point of being in business if you don't keep ahead of the field?'

Susan wished they hadn't started off like this. As Cleeve sat on the settee beside her, she feared losing control.

'You win, Cleeve,' she admitted, hoping to steer the conversation eventually to where she wanted, 'you always do.'

'I didn't with you: you left me, remember?' Cleeve said, taking a large drink.

'Too much competition, Cleeve. I gave you the choice: you could keep your wife but you had to give up the other girls. You didn't: you couldn't, that was your answer, take it or leave it.'

'I don't care how you put it, Susan, you left me. Not many do, but *you* did: and I respect you for that.'

'Really? You respect me so much that you went with my little sister?'

'I didn't know you were related until later: when I found out it was too late: we had already done the business.'

'And so you kept on doing it?'

'It takes two, you know: Helen didn't object: she wanted it as much as me. I never forced myself on her, she knows her own mind.'

'She's a child, Cleeve, she's just eighteen.'

'She's old enough to know what she wants, believe me.'

He said this in the way a man might boast of a casual conquest to his drunken friends, and Susan felt sick.

'My goodness, Cleeve, don't you ever stop and wonder?' she asked. 'Don't you sometimes ask yourself what it would be like it if it was your daughter Chanteuse? Don't you imagine how *you* would feel?'

'The world is a dangerous place, Susan, people have to fend for themselves.'

'So if Chanteuse came home one evening and said she was pregnant, you would be comfortable with that?'

'I won't be pleased, but at the end of the day if you act like a woman you have to bear the pain like a woman.'

'You're just saying that.'

'No, I mean it: if Chanteuse is woman enough to "take man" then what can I do?'

'You would just sit back and let her behave like that?'

'It's her life.'

'You wouldn't say anything to her?'

'I wouldn't be over the moon. But if she has to learn the hard way, so be it.'

'So you wouldn't get mad with her? You wouldn't throw her out? You wouldn't tell her about the disgrace she was bringing on the family?'

'I wouldn't like it,' Cleeve repeated, like a man who thought this so remote he could give any old answer. 'I wouldn't be thrilled but what could I do? Chanteuse is nineteen. Next year she's going to England to study Public Administration: if she is stupid enough to set her life back ten years then that is *her* problem.'

'Cleeve, you used to be honest with me, but now you can't even be bothered to answer me like an adult. I knew you were a cheat but I didn't realise that you had taken up lying as well. Who was it who threatened Chanteuse's boyfriend and warned him to keep away from her earlier in the year?'

Cleeve poured himself another whisky, drank deeply, then roared with laughter.

'So you heard, did you?' he asked, unable to suppress the laughter.

'Yes,' Susan replied, 'everyone heard about the way you threatened Joel Prospero.'

' I was only trying to see if he had real feelings for her, or if he was just after her money.'

'And that was all there was to it?'

'Yes: I made some discreet enquiries and I found out he was a nice young man from an educated family.'

'And you settled for that?'

'Yes. They're not rich but they're ambitious. He has a sister studying Pharmacy and a brother taking his Law finals. Chanteuse could do a lot worse.'

'And my sister? Where does that leave Helen?'

'I will look after the baby.'

'You are happy for her to put you down as the father on the birth certificate?'

'I will pay the maintenance.'

'That's what being a father is about, is it?'

'I'm a married man, Susan, I have a wife and two children, nineteen and seventeen. I do my bit, I maintain my children. But I can't have more than one wife. I would take out the child publicly if I could, but it's not so easy as you well know: SVG is a small place, suppose my wife finds out?'

'And she doesn't know about all your other children? She's got no idea about your other women?'

'My wife is too sensible to listen to rumours. Call her aloof, call her foolish, but that's how she is. She has her legal practice, she's too busy with her own life. When I'm not away on business

I'm beside her every night. I buy her whatever she wants, I drive her to her beloved church every Sunday. When she goes shopping in New York I pay for the trip. I buy the children whatever they need and, without boasting, I keep her happy in bed.'

'You make it sound so simple.'

'My life *is* simple: if you get involved with me you have to play the way I play. If you don't like it you leave: that's what you did, isn't it?'

'So you don't really have any feelings for any of these girls? You didn't have any feelings for me?'

'Of course I had feelings for you: I always knew there was something special about you. *You* left me, remember? Not many did that. I tried to introduce you to whisky, you wouldn't touch it. Brandy, no. Barbados, to see horseracing: you wouldn't come with me. I offered you a job with a generous salary as my personal secretary, you preferred to slave in a bank, working your way up through the ranks! You wouldn't dance for me, you wouldn't take part in my show. Still, if I was a younger man, or if you were closer to my age, who knows, eh?'

'That's just whisky talk, Cleeve.'

'I'm serious.'

'You wouldn't know the meaning of the word. You won't have a clue. You're so accustomed to getting what you want you never stop to consider anyone else's feelings. If I didn't leave you, you would have got rid of me. Two months, three, it was just a matter of time. I was just another girl with a good figure. You have no idea how I felt afterwards. It took me ages to get over the feeling that I was just one of the crop. Marry *me*, Cleeve? No chance, that was never going to happen. But it doesn't matter now.'

'I would, Susan, I would have married you.'

'You're only saying that because you can't have me anymore. Because I had the courage to walk away.'

'No, Susan, I would have married you, because you have something the others didn't have: fight. You know how to stand on your own two feet.'

'I was just the latest in your collection, admit it, it's sad but it's true. I was fortunate though, I quickly realised the kind of man you are. Why did you have to tell Helen about us? What kind of a man does that? Do you know how I felt hearing my little sister reciting all the things that are supposed to remain private between two people?'

'I'm sorry, Susan,' Cleeve said, although his voice didn't contain a trace of it. 'You know how it is when you're close to someone on a hot night with a good brandy by your side: you say things you later regret.'

'You don't know the meaning of the word, Cleeve. With your money and connections, I'm sure you've never regretted anything in your whole life.'

'Look, Susan, I'm tired. It's been a hard day. Come round next Thursday and we'll talk things over, all right?'

'I don't think so,' Susan replied firmly.

'Well in that case, will you do me one last favour and drive me home? I'm tired and I've had a little too much whisky. I can't go with these country roads this time of night.'

'Why should I?' Susan asked.

'For old times' sake?'

'Why not,' Susan said, after thinking it over for a while, 'why not?'

She would drop him off, she decided, she hadn't visited the windward side of the island for months. She would take him home and spend the night at her aunt's house in Caratal. No harm in that, was there?

As she slid into the car, Susan was glad she had cleared the air with Cleeve. Knowing that he had no hold over her, she could face Helen now. But it was clear he had no intention of maintaining her child. The occasional twenty-dollar bill would be the best she could hope for. It was the way men like him operated, publicly, and by gestures. A pat on the head, two crisp notes, the public display witnessed by an afternoon crowd, the boastful acknowledgement of a son or daughter whose features they forgot the moment they climbed into their vehicle on the way to the next village.

Still, Helen would cope. Young and intelligent, she would get the second chance she deserved. Having got over Cleeve, having rediscovered the exhilaration of mastering Chemistry and Physics, she would struggle to recognise the gullible teenager named Helen Wiley.

Susan drove for twenty-five minutes, the scent of the hot night wafting to her, the soft roar of the sea soothing and reassuring. With only the night for company, there was no conversation now. Exhausted, drunk, Cleeve reclined in the front seat, a smile on his lips, like a man in the middle of a long delightful dream. Just as well, she told herself, she didn't care for his talk. For what was left to talk about?

She thought of all the village girls who had fallen under his spell, the families wrecked, the girlhood ambitions thwarted. Mere trophies, what wreckage in search of new sexual treasures!

At twenty-two, the myth powerful, the impulse to be the one to tame him irresistible, she too had been taken in. Money and notoriety were too powerful a lure to resist, but, thank goodness, she had found a way out.

Through the darkness she drove, slowly, cautiously, few vehicles travelling in either direction at that late hour. She felt at peace with herself, her love of the countryside revived by the cleansing meeting Cleeve. There was a sweetness to the breeze, a softness that mimicked the gentleness of light rain on the roof. She loved this tract of the island, rugged, scenic. Attuned to its smells, she loved its contours, the road perilously close to the sea, she loved the warm smiles of its people.

As she drove through the tunnel at Byera there was a moaning and chuntering sound like a man being hounded in his dream.

'Stop the car,' Cleeve roared like a wounded bear, 'stop the blasted car, let me out: call of nature.'

Susan drove through the village, past Black Point, past the turning to Chester Cottage, until she found a suitable spot to stop, away from houses. On the hill that gradually descends from Black Point to Grand Sable, she slowly brought the car to rest. Cleeve pushed open the passenger door and, a few moments later, Susan heard him relieving himself noisily in the gutter through a series of moans and grunts. Eventually, his belt undone, he staggered back to the car and yanked open the rear door.

'I'm going in the back,' he growled, the stink of urine enveloping him, 'more space. Wake me up when you're nearly home.'

He dragged himself noisily into the back seat, cursing and swearing at what, it wasn't clear to Susan, and within two minutes, had begun to snore. That was when the idea came to her. She didn't know its source, or why it had chosen that moment, but the suggestion was so compelling, the implication so delicious that she had no doubt about its execution. She didn't think of consequences, her own, her family's, his. The moment was everything. She had to obey, or she would never forgive herself.

She brought the car to a gentle stop and looked in the back of the car to check his condition. Still snoring, totally out of it. She eased out of the car, turned off the lights, and placed her handbag carefully by the roadside. There were no vehicles approaching in either direction. Good. She returned to the car. She had a final look at Cleeve's sleeping bulk in the back, saw and heard him heaving like a giant boar. Good.

She manoeuvred the car to the right hand side of the road so that it was facing the levelled coconut field seven hundred metres below. The engine humming softly, she slowly released the handbrake. She closed her eyes, took a huge breath, and asked to be forgiven. A gentle push at the rear of the car, then she stepped back. She watched the car plunge over the bank, uncertainly at first then, gathering speed, in a violent, thumping metallic rhythm.

In the days when sugar was king, they shipped molasses and rum at Grand Sable. On rough days, when Byera Bay was calm, through the Black Point Tunnel they trekked with their precious cargo bound for England. A tiny island strutting on the world stage, SVG played its role to perfection.

This history has been forgotten, even by those who live at Grand Sable and neighbouring Georgetown. They know each tree intimately, the depth and temperature of the river are second nature to residents. They spend hours studying the habits of the Caribbean Sea, raging one day, alluring the next. People see a once-flourishing coconut field levelled for picnics on bank holidays, they enjoy the trek through Black Point Tunnel with its ancient secrets. This land is too ordinary for history, they feel, this segment of country couldn't have supported heroes or permitted suffering.

When the explosion of the car was no more, Susan placed her bag over her shoulder and began the walk home to her aunt Judy in Caratal, three miles away. Cleeve's demise wouldn't be history, but a short bitter chapter.

At dawn people would rush to stare at the twisted wreck of the vehicle, wedged between ancient trees that had witnessed so much. Cleeve would soon be forgotten, but one day people open their eyes to the majesty of Black Point, and the history of the region will resurface.

the circuit

In the glorious summer of 1976, with England under siege from the fiery blades of the West Indian batsmen, Cunningham invited six friends to a do at his flat on Givens Court. Forty-six, short and square-shaped, he was known for his generosity. Single by default, his time was his own. Nell Young, who claimed to despise him as much as he hated her, had left him a week earlier, and hell would freeze before he had her back!

'You crossing the point of no return, Nell,' he had warned her. 'Once you close that front door, don't set foot here again!'

He wasn't thinking of Nell now. The heat of the August sun on his back as he polished his beloved Triumph Herald, a quiet celebration of his ten years in England was the only thing on his mind.

He loved England, especially on summer Saturdays that enticed you into the car and suggested driving for the sheer hell of it. The turquoise Triumph gleaming like new, a spin to blow away the winter cobwebs seemed perfectly natural. Off he sped, then, down the A40 to London, heading east to his favourite spot, the windows lowered, the warm air assaulting his prominent forehead.

A slight miscalculation landed him in Hounslow, and an altercation with a cyclist in Finchley further delayed his arrival at his destination, Shepherd's Bush. That was Cunningham. With him things were seldom straightforward. Nothing wrong with a little detour, he consoled himself as he walked briskly to the market, only those without a sense of adventure drive directly from A to B, and promptly back.

There was his friend, Felix Findlay, for instance. Get in his way on the motorway and he was all horns and flashing headlights. Nestling behind God's back, pretty villages like Fingest and Naphill were a blur to him. Thank goodness, he wasn't like Felix who resented taking a wrong turn. Who, after fifteen years in the old Country, could get you to Birmingham in an hour, but was blind to the delights of the Buckinghamshire countryside!

Not that Cunningham knew many places. But there was one he knew extremely well: Shepherd's Bush. Food, drink and music under one roof, the bustling simplicity of the market was like a magnet. A 'semi- regular' at the Caribbean record shop opposite the tube station, he had once blown a week's wages on five Jamaican pre-releases. Rare, exclusive discs with wacky labels that remained dormant for years before becoming public, they were his pride and joy, spun when Nell visited, or for his friends, Woods, Humphrey and Morrel.

The proprietor, Mikey Mills, was a Dominican with a striking white beard. He had once come third in a comedy show, he liked to boast, the next time he bound to win. The moment Cunningham stepped into the shop, Mikey came forward to greet him.

'Graham, old boy,' he said, taking Cunningham by the elbow, 'long time no see: what happen, the missus have you under manners?'

'Cunningham,' Cunningham corrected him. 'How many times I have to tell you that Mikey? You can't remember a simple Caribbean name?'

'So Graham was your maiden name, was it?' Mikey asked, removing his arm now that Cunningham was in the shop proper.

'Stick to selling records, Mikey,' Cunningham replied, 'you're not funny: see what happen to your beard?'

'You never see a black man with a white beard before?' Mikey asked, stroking the beard proudly.

'Not on a thirty-year old.'

'My whiskers upset you?'

'No: it just make you look like a Uranian.'

'You prejudice or something, old boy? You don't believe black and white should mix?'

'I just wonder what turn your beard white, Mikey, young man like you: must be *some juice* you feeding it.'

'Forget the bush,' said Mikey, feeling that Cunningham was getting the better of him, 'what you after this time?'

'The usual.'

'Music for a party?'

'Just having a few friends round,' Cunningham replied.

'What's the address?'

'*Friends*,' said Cunningham, 'I said *friends*.'

'What's on the menu?'

'Nothing special: food, music, rum.'

'Sure you don't need someone to keep things swinging?'

'Leave your number: if I get desperate I'll send a pigeon.'

'You need some big-people music then?'

'Naturally.'

'You're in luck: I have some new Sparrow, and a Percy Sledge LP to break any woman heart.'

'No woman heart to break,' Cunningham was serious for the first time.

'Be brave, Cunningham,' Mikey laid a mock sympathetic hand on Cunningham's shoulder. 'Go and ask her back. Beg if you have to: women don't mind a man begging.'

'Not this man. Now, fetch my music.'

Mikey ducked under the counter and emerged, a moment later, with two LPs.

'Here,' he said, offering them to Cunningham, '£5 for the Sparrow and you can have the Sledge for £4.50.'

Cunningham paid with a ten pound note and headed for the door.

'Your change, Graham,' Mikey called after him, 'you forget your change.'

'Keep it,' Cunningham suggested, 'buy yourself an ice cream.'

Cunningham hurried to the butcher, then found a Ghanaian woman who sold ground provisions. Resisting the urge to haggle, within ten minutes he had secured the ingredients for his soup. The car loaded, he took off for home not long after. Pointing the

Triumph west, in the direction of Oxford, his fingers crossed, he prayed that his luck held.

Callaloo soup, Cunningham said to himself later that afternoon, as he trimmed the stalks, what could better callaloo soup? Rich and warming, soft, the tripe melting with each dainty bite, he could almost taste it. 'Old talk', Caribbean food, rum and good company, was there a better way of passing a gorgeous evening?

If they were good guests, he pledged, if they could detect the hint of ginger in the soup, he might explain the system he had used to pick the winner in the 3.10 at Ascot! As he dusted and polished, the sun streaming in through the windows, he had no idea what he was starting.

For each guest brought a friend, the friend an acquaintance, the acquaintance a mate, and before he knew it, like the farmer in the den, the husband taking a wife, the wife a maid, the maid a nurse, each adding inexorably to the chain, the settee was creaking. Like a stranded fish, Cunningham's mouth snapped open as the numbers multiplied. He was being shunted from pillar to post. If he wasn't careful, he sensed, things could quickly get out of control.

He was on good terms with the neighbours. The flats were home to those who were single by choice or by cruel fate. But did that give old Klein Henry the right to use his cooker? And wasn't that Nell sharing roti and souse as though she was the hostess?

Dark in winter and autumn, the kitchen was on the immediate left as you entered the flat. It could accommodate three men with their hands in their pockets comfortably, but not the throng now exchanging greetings like guests at a wedding reception. Cunningham grinned weakly.

The flat had been hastily tidied, patches of condensation were cruelly exposed. It was far too small for an ambush. Above the din, as he fixed Melda Reeves a cocktail, he heard the gramophone choking on an alien record, the volume increased to a level he feared would separate the wooden accoutrement from its elderly legs. He had had enough, something had to be done.

Like a cane-cutter on commission he parted the crowd, distributing roughly those in his way. The culprits, a teenage couple from Coventry, weren't hard to find. Having turned up the volume, they were winding outrageously as though they had forgotten where they were. Enraged by their cheek, Cunningham yanked the arm of the record player from the disc. The music aborted, and the two dancers froze like children playing musical chairs.

'Helllllllo,' Cunningham called out, 'Yvette, Nezil, can I have your attention please!'

The disappearance of the music didn't have the desired impact. If anything, conversation increased. There was shouting and laughter and Cunningham felt the joke was on him.

'Hello,' he hollered, holding up the offending LP, 'everybody, I said, "Will you damn well listen!"'

A sudden hush came over the room and all eyes looked in his direction.

'Thank you,' Cunningham said, slowly lowering the record. 'Thanks for coming. But as you can see, 47 Givens Court isn't The Ritz. It's comfortable for a bachelor, but too small for more than *six* people. I want you to have a good time. But please consider the neighbours. And mind the carpet!'

He had spoken from the centre of the room, surrounded by a sea of anxious black faces. Having given them a licence to enjoy themselves, conversation resumed, but gradually. Taking advantage of this, Nell, who constantly accused him of being good for only one thing, although she couldn't remember what it was, sidled up to him.

She took his free arm and linked hers, as though they were man and wife. Cunningham was confused. Nell was starting something he wasn't sure he could finish. He had banned her from the flat, yet here she was tying up him up in knots!

'Good evening everyone,' Nell said, in the pretty voice Cunningham loved and detested simultaneously, 'welcome to our summer soiree. The winter was so cold, for months I didn't see a smiling Caribbean face. That is why me and Cunningham organised this little function. You all know Cunningham, but I know him better than any of you: and I mean you too, Susan Seaton. What he meant to say is that everyone's welcome. So eat, drink and be merry. And enjoy yourselves like is your last day on earth!'

She turned to Cunningham, smiled, then kissed him on the lips.

'Christ,' Cunningham thought, 'what the hell is this woman doing?'

That Sunday afternoon, as he crawled out of bed, his tongue coarse and heavy, his head refusing to accompany his body to the fridge for the glass of water Nell had requested, Cunningham swore that he would be more careful next time: if West Indians couldn't comprehend that six doesn't equal forty-five, then they would have to find an alternative venue to cut loose. Further, if Nell believed she had got the better of him with her public performance and her sleeping over, she had underestimated him: she had rejected him too often. Single he was, and that was how it was going to remain!

Reeling from the shock, the hasty pledge to distance himself seemed as natural as the sting of winter. As Nell cleared away glasses, bottles and plates, he didn't wish to see another West Indian foot inside his flat for a year. To the 'lavettes' who had gatecrashed, to those seeking relief from the drudgery of the chocolate factory and the hum of the paper mill, Givens Court was strictly out of bounds!

For their town, small, but close to London, wasn't exactly bereft of night life, he would remind anyone brazen enough to pay him another visit. Of an evening there were pubs and clubs to cater for every taste. Home to an armoury of Jamaican sound-systems, Newlands Club, situated under the flyover, swung till a satanic five every Saturday. *Quaker City* from Birmingham easily registering on the Richter scale, youngsters could have no complaints.

Young and old were welcome at Newlands, but not at Kings Drive, two miles from the town centre off the London Road. Seated menacingly at the entrance, the muscular proprietor, Venol Marshall, strictly enforced the 'Adults Only' policy. Sweaty, funky and smoky, the basement was crammed with worshippers of late nights. A mad week at work, a frosty Saturday at home? Then Kings Drive was the place to go.

There, husbands danced with wives until early dawn when, their smiles adjusted, they returned home to their snoring partners and loving families. Single or free, obeying the night code of absolute secrecy, revellers danced their cares away. Take your pick, Cunningham had mumbled to the uninvited guests as they collected their belongings, go to Newlands, or sleep at Kings Drive: but get Givens Court out of your mind!

The weekend after his do, while pressing his 'earthman' trousers for an incursion into Watford, Woods, Morrel and Humphrey arrived with 'sincere apologies' for the liberties they had taken, two 'women friends' from Luton, and enough rum to power a small car. The invasion of Watford was postponed and, as the brandy lightened his head and the younger woman nibbled his left ear, The Circuit was born. Cunningham's bachelor life had found a purpose. For the next seven years, consumed by The Circuit, his Saturday nights would be solidly booked.

Cunningham, Morrel, Woods and Humphrey formed the core. Organising and coaxing, they whipped members into line. Below them was a second tier of members, happily-married men and women who drifted in and out according to their partner's mood, and 'free agents' who thought nothing of rolling in at eight on a Sunday morning. For seven glorious years The Circuit would provide a meeting place for those who loved all things Caribbean.

The Circuit wasn't exactly a club. To call it an organisation is like calling a pet cat a cheetah. It was a loose association without leader, secretary or treasurer. There were no officials, although Cunningham and Woods conducted a brief initiation. Members paid no tithe, there was no obligation to attend the weekly gathering. If you had other business and arrived at two, no one raised an eyebrow.

This arrangement suited the temperament of its members. Saturday after Saturday, collecting at a different home, rotating the obligation to provide for the membership, they congregated with religious fervour. Trinidadians got to know Dominicans, Jamaicans heard and understood, for the first time, the accents of the Eastern Caribbean.

Ten was a fair turn out, on a good night a raucous nineteen. Pouring out the experiences of the week or recalling a favourite Anansi story, they shared everything. A warm welcome awaited guests from Essex, Luton, Reading and Oxford. For those people nostalgic for the sun and sea, for people obsessed with the past and indifferent to the present or future, The Circuit was home for a night.

The items on the agenda changed little. A meal was expected, the choice resting with the host, a deck of cards, a pack of dominoes or some long-forgotten Caribbean game such as Wari. Occasionally, a member brought along a book of short stories or read some poetry, but conversation, anecdotes, singing, and food were the constants. To keep the evening flowing, there was liquor from every Caribbean island.

Since attendance wasn't compulsory, the numbers varied. The core was dedicated but not all members were as diligent. In the bitter winter of 1979, Cunningham, Morrel and Woods were forced to declare a 'short Circuit'. Three might be a crowd, they pronounced haughtily, but it certainly was no company. At 11:30 they had halted proceedings. Home they had crawled, grumpy and deflated, in bed on the left side of midnight for the first time in years.

The weather could disrupt proceedings, the group also had

to concede to big events. Talk of a big 'fete' in London in 1980, with a live Caribbean band and the promise of an unforgettable night on the dance floor, had the town buzzing. West Indian women all dressed up, their perfume maddening, their movements bewitching, nights like this delivered their promise.

'Got to take Clara,' Woods announced the week before, 'the wife need to renew her annual dance-MOT. She don't get out much these days, but she like to know she still have the moves in her.'

'My Doris going too,' Humphrey added, 'she not one for dancing, but she like to soak up the atmosphere.'

'You taking Nell, I assume,' Woods said to Cunningham.

'Of course,' Cunningham lied, 'she already choose her outfit.'

Excusing himself there and then, Cunningham sped to Nell's house. Letting himself in, he found her lying on the settee reading Derek Walcott, her neat ankles exposed, her hair plaited in fine, tight circles, exposing the delicate ears.

'Nell,' he began, a little sheepishly, 'how things?'

'Things good,' Nell replied, without looking up. 'What you doing here?'

'Just come to see how you are.'

'Really?' she said, with a low disbelieving sigh.

'You know, Nell,' said Cunningham, 'you look as pretty as that first day at Heathrow.'

'What you want Cunningham?' Nell closed the volume and sat up. 'What you after?'

'What happen Nell, you forget how to accept a compliment?'

'I'm a woman Cunningham, not a girl.'

'So if you looking nice, you don't want me to say?'

'Tell Susan Seaton: *she* always fishing for compliments and you always dishing them out: and that's not all you giving her, from what I hear.'

'Rumours, Nell: just gossip.'

'If you say so, Cunningham. Now, what you want?'

'There's a big dance in London next Saturday: fancy it?'

'Who playing?'

'A band from Martinique.'

'And you leave it so late to ask me? One week's notice, that's all I'm worth?'

'Foundry-work is hard, you know: most days I fall asleep the moment I get home.'

'I'll think about it Cunningham. You don't come round for three weeks and you expect me to give up my evening just like that?'

'You want me to keep away from you, you want me to visit: make your mind up Nell, will you?'

'Cunningham, do you have to believe everything I tell you? How many times you banned me from Givens Court? Ten, fifteen, twenty? Do you turn me away when I arrive?'

'No.'

'Exactly. Now you give me one week's notice like a landlord! When am I going to find time to buy a dress? I'm a black woman, Cunningham, where can I find a hairdresser between now and next Friday? Take a Cressex girl, take Susan, or one of your Luton friends. Try me again in 1985.'

Off they had headed then to Stratford, all five squeezed into Humphrey's car, The Circuit adjourned, Cunningham feeling like a fool. The following Saturday, they had reassembled to discuss the ways of men and women, and the pleasures of a good dance.

Membership thrived. Through habit, through dedication. Like an extended family, a good night was always guaranteed. Disagreements never grew into an argument. Even under the influence of hot nights and strong liquor, no one went home with a grudge. Cunningham lived for Saturday, The Circuit was his Nell Young.

Three bottles stood on the wooden coffee table, four, if you included the 'dead' bottle of *Martell* Norman Ifill had been instructed to remove to make way for the coffee Cunningham had ordered. He eyed the 1.5 litre bottle of *Sunset,* 'Very Strong Rum', as the label warned, but decided against a final shot.

The cold penetrating his cotton shirt, he had had enough. Without his noticing, the music had faded. On his left, he heard Osmond Blake muttering to himself about the diluted vodka he had been served. Snoring softly in a corner, fresh from the cold, Samuel Tall, was already out for the count. It was time to call a halt to these late nights, Cunningham decided, he was either getting old or he needed fresh company.

The Circuit used to be such fun! For seven years it made the hell-hole of a foundry bearable. His back aching, numb limbs begging him to find another job, the thought of distant pleasures always pulled him through. But the old 'bachelor boys' and 'single girls' had dispersed, or had resigned their membership. Each year a trickle returned to the Caribbean to fulfil their childhood dreams. He saluted his former companions. The

Circuit would live on, he promised, he would do his best to uphold its traditions.

With tears in his eyes, Cunningham had driven Cuthbert Sutton and his wife, Doreen, to Gatwick one week, only to repeat the journey with Woods and Clara a fortnight later.

'A room waiting for you in Barbados,' Clara had reminded him, in the rich Bajan accent thirty years in England couldn't erase. 'The moment you phone, we at the airport.'

The Woods to Barbados, the Butes to SVG, others to Trinidad and Tobago and Antigua, retired couples apprehensive like honeymooners, Cunningham was left behind with his single life. Embracing The Circuit, he had never settled down. Nell dropped by occasionally, and their birthdays, Christmas and Easter together, were sacrosanct. But as he lingered over the *Sunset*, Cunningham began to wonder if that was all there was to his life.

The twitchiness that drove him from his home every Saturday night was still there, but the new members depressed him. Fresh off the plane or recently initiated, the young men and women had little conversation. Their stories were dull or vicious, one had halted Cunningham in the middle of an Anansi story to catch the football scores. The traditions of the Circuit? It was their time now, they didn't care about the past.

Within a month of joining, twenty-five year old Anne-Jean Moore had proposed a vote on introducing gambling and smoking, her younger sister, Jean-Anne, had suggested enlivening proceedings with a stripper! Receiving no support, the pair had stripped down to their underwear as they played dominoes. He had a fight on his hands, Cunningham knew, it was them or him.

Too many of the men were like Godfrey Goodluck, he reflected, they couldn't take their licks, they didn't know the art of compromising with women. Tall and handsome, Godfrey despised everyone and everything. His long neck slowly retracting into his collar, before he had knocked back his third brandy, the devastation that was his home life with his wife, Marsha, would be rehashed in a pitiful performance. Like a man who needed to purge himself, their conversations would be replayed to the members, and her 'sins' exposed. Her 'fancy man' had bought her a car and a new wardrobe, what was their mortgage agreement?

What in the world is new, Cunningham asked himself that cold Saturday night, how many pathetic stories should a man have to put up with? Home life belonged at home, the Circuit wasn't a judge! He would get out, he decided, he would resign his membership. This young bunch was too much for him. He didn't understand them, he had no desire to.

At the far end of the room a couple was dancing although the music had been turned off and the television switched on for the racing results. He had to go: no way could he remain with people who danced to their own quiet humming. Refusing the rum, Cunningham grabbed his keys, grunted goodnight to those who were still conscious, and reached for his coat.

Sundays can be empty, Saturdays long and depressing. After quitting The Circuit Cunningham didn't know what to do with his time. He slept through the weekend like a patient prescribed rest by his doctor. He felt old and redundant. The temptation to drive to the gathering was strong. A stern lecture, and he was sure The Circuit would be reclaimed. But no. Cut your losses, he told himself, be a man: once you leave, never go back. When he feared a fourth week of numbing emptiness, he remembered that Nell's birthday was coming up.

Cunningham had lodged with Nell for a month immediately after his arrival in England. His first job, in a supermarket, was due to her. She drove him to work and picked him up after his shift. She introduced him to Woods, she helped to secure his work papers. They became friends, they were soon more than friends.

A year later, she moved in with Cunningham for a 'trial'. For a week they lived like a couple, taking the train to London, shopping at Shepherd's Bush market, going to the cinema. A trip to Windsor Castle via Basingstoke had exposed his driving, Nell had had to take control. Nell was obsessed with her hair, Cunningham learned to be patient. Declaring the trial a success, Cunningham went to the local TSB, drew out fifty pounds and offered it to Nell as she was packing to leave.

'Cunningham,' Nell said in a voice that haunted him for months, 'you remember telling me I didn't know anything about men? And how I have no maternal feelings? Well, learn this lesson from me: never give a woman money. If she asks for a dollar, buy her a nice blouse. For a pound, get her a silver bracelet instead. Some perfume was all I was expecting, not your money.'

Cunningham arrived at Sobers Avenue with a silver necklace and a gold watch he was confident Nell would appreciate. Her hair greying at the front and sides, her brown eyes soft, she had clearly lost none of her beauty. What was the matter with them, he asked himself, why, after so many years, was there a line they couldn't cross together?

He offered the presents and watched Nell's face light up like a girl's at Christmas. A kiss for the necklace and another for the watch, and Cunningham wished he had bought a pair of earrings and a pair of soft brown leather shoes to complement the softness of her skin!

'The necklace is beautiful, Cunningham,' Nell said, 'and the watch is gorgeous.'

'For you, Nell, anything,' Cunningham replied expansively.

'You mean that?'

'Deadly serious.'

'Where did you buy them?'

'London.'

'Shepherd's Bush?'

'Oxford Street.'

'Oxford Street, Cunningham? You? How?'

'Don't ask.'

'You did that for me? You drove to the West End?'

'Well, not quite.'

'What then?'

'I took the tube from the Bush.'

'Just for my birthday presents?'

'Yes.'

'Well,' Nell declared, 'my my.'

Returning the gifts to their boxes, she then made for the kitchen and Cunningham followed.

'You're early,' she said, 'I haven't prepared anything.'

'Why don't we go to a restaurant instead?' Cunningham suggested.

Nell thought for a while then said, 'Nah, I want a nice relaxing day.'

'Sure I can't tempt you?'

'No: Oh the joys of getting old!'

'We're all getting old Nell.'

'Some faster than others. You still look good for 53: I'm 49 and I feel more like 55.'

'Well, you look as radiant now as the day you and Woods collected me at the airport,' Cunningham laid it on thick.

'Stop it,' Nell giggled, 'rope in the sweet talk: save it for the women at The Circuit.'

'The Circuit break up,' Cunningham said sadly.

'What,' Nell asked, 'The Circuit smash?'

'Some of the new crop still meet up, but I resign. They out to destroy everything The Circuit stand for.'

'What a shame,' Nell offered her sympathy.

'I know. But it's your birthday, forget The Circuit. Now, what you want to do?'

'Let's go for a drive.'

Cunningham watched Nell mount the stairs with the presents. Hers was an easy, graceful walk. He knew it well, would recognise it even when he was in decline. 16 Sobers Avenue had been his home, and that homely feel still pervaded it. It had been modernised, yet it retained the warmth of a home based on simple good taste. A framed picture of his first winter in England stood on the bookcase, and there were others of their trips together to Wales and Blackpool. He had moved out, but he had never truly left.

They drove to Oxford, visited the natural history museum, then went shopping. On the way back Cunningham's early exit from the A40 landed them in Aylesbury. Nell suggested a visit to his cousin, Thomas Drakes. A seventy-five year old widower, Thomas brewed three cups of weak tea.

'Now,' he said after his first sip, 'I see you two still together!'

Nell and Cunningham grunted at the same time.

'So many people divorcing these days,' the old man thwacked his lips, 'it's a miracle to find an old couple.'

Cunningham kept his cup fixed between his lips to avoid answering and, searching the room with her eyes for an ally, Nell settled on the curtains.

'The house still nice and cosy, Thomas,' she said, 'and those curtains, what lively patterns and unusual colours!'

'Special offer,' Thomas replied proudly. 'Bicester 1976: and they still going strong. The children flee the nest, but the curtains still standing: quality, eh?'

'The children well?' Cunningham asked to steer the conversation away from themselves.

'Both through university,' Thomas replied, 'Psychology, Chemistry: those children have my brain. Now, how long since you two married?'

'We're not *exactly* married,' Nell answered, choosing the tone carefully.

'After all this time?' Thomas took another sip of tea and grimaced at its bitterness.

'We're friends,' Nell said.

'Just friends?' the old man frowned. 'Men and women can't be just friends!'

'Me and Nell have a special relationship,' Cunningham explained.

'Cunningham,' Thomas grumbled, 'I thought you had more

sense than that. You call yourself a cousin and you don't know this basic law? You either have a relationship or you don't: now, which is it?'

'It's getting late,' Nell said. 'Drink up, Cunningham, time to get going.'

After escaping, they drove in silence for a while then Nell said, 'What a crazy old man.'

'Old Thomas?' Cunningham replied, 'he went off ages ago.'

'I hope madness doesn't run in the family.'

'It start and end with Thomas.'

They both chucked then Nell asked, 'What you going to do now The Circuit smash?'

'I don't know,' Cunningham replied, 'I miss the meetings, but it's time to move on.'

'To what?'

'I don't know.'

'What about you and me forming our own Circuit?' Nell proposed.

'Not enough members to go round.'

'I meant with just me and you Cunningham.'

'You mean you visit me one week and I visit you the next?'

'No Cunningham, don't make things so complicated.'

'What you mean then?'

'A Circuit with just the two of us.'

'You think that will work?'

'No harm in another trial: move in for a month and we'll take it from there. It would be like The Circuit every day.'

'Remember the last time,' Cunningham reminded her, 'one good week then everything crash!'

'We're older and wiser now.'

'You're sure about that?'

'We're older then, Cunningham, if not wiser.'

'What's in it for me?' Cunningham asked.

'Me,' Nell answered. 'Isn't that enough?'

'I couldn't ask for more. But where's *your* percentage?'

'You.'

'And you satisfy with that?'

'It's a start.'

When they were married a year later, Cunningham wondered who or what had driven them together.

basil lincoln

The government shave the terraced face of the cliffs at Sans Souci to widen the road, yet is easy to bypass Mount Greenan on the journey from Kingstown to country. A pity, a real pity. For although it bring back painful memories, is a village I love dearly. To go past without stopping is like a godparent crossing the road to avoid sponsoring their godchild a dollar. But I mustn't joke.

Debbie Crichton, a close friend, come from there. She at university in Cuba now, fluent in Spanish and English as well as Vincy. Clever on top of good-looking, what a girl! Our friendship blossom as waitresses in *Gregory's* Restaurant. Until nine months ago I was still serving at the restaurant and helping out in the kitchen, but sooner or later everyone have to move on in life.

Debbie single-minded and ambitious but I was born cautious. From a girl she set her heart on medicine, nothing, no one else in the picture. Adelphi Primary, Girls High, Community College, it seem only natural when she win a prestigious island scholarship. Content to dress up, sit and read all day and pray for tomorrow, for me was one soppy novel after another.

Tongue-in-cheek, Debbie suggest teaching, banking, the police, librarian, occupations in SVG that allow ample time for reading. Not for me, I answer, none of them catch my fancy. She coax and encourage, beg me even. Still no. One Easter, on an excursion to Bequia, she finally convince me to apply for a post at Clare Valley Public Library. A week later, surrounded by inky newspapers and dusty paperbacks, I sitting pretty behind an ancient wooden desk as Assistant Librarian!

Naturally, that call for a celebration! So we spend the following Saturday night at her house toasting my success with a cook-up, chicken with noodles, and plenty of tannias and young bananas. And, like an old married couple, we 'hook up', link arms, as we skip to the Methodist church in the early morning. The Wednesday Debbie depart to study medicine I didn't cry, but I was like a fish out of water. She might be 3000 miles overseas, but my love for Mount Greenan could never fade.

Partitioned by a tiny stream that perish in the baking sand before it reach the sea, the church on the eastern bank of the village stand overlooking the main road. Tall and proud, a grey concrete shell during the week, the church truly come alive on Sundays. Such joyful and uplifting singing. Since the age of fourteen the love of churches with me, I must have worshipped in every single one in the parish of St David.

Lorna Toney is the last person to disparage a faith or ridicule their customs. The Anglican church in Bridgetown, the Baptist church in Richland Park, I attended both in the November of my eighteenth birthday as a special treat. Tranquil and humbling, even now just sitting in a church can fill my eyes with tears. After the congregation depart the Baptist church, I kneel and pray: for a long life, for my parents, to get married, to find a job with good prospects. And I feel sure is because of prayer why Basil Lincoln couldn't truly touch me.

Strolling home one Friday afternoon after work, admiring the old church in Mount Greenan, I hear a man screaming. I should have carried on walking. Instead, I stop to investigate. Big mistake, big, big mistake. Nineteen at the time, too young to spot danger, like a pumpkin fritter into hot oil, I drop right in.

Still, I have to count myself lucky. No one I know personally endure what I endure and live to tell the tale. Imagine that, a whole night in Basil Lincoln company, me and him alone in the house! How I escape, and why, is still a mystery.

'Trust no man,' my mother used to caution me often. 'But most of all, watch out for Basil Lincoln. Mess with that man and your life over.'

The warning, a joke but with a serious purpose, I used to laugh off. Who you telling to shun bad company, I would reply, isn't that second nature to any girl with a little ambition? Allowing a man to greet you by the waist is for girls like Camille Crozier who secretly like to play, but not for me. A LIAT pilot was brazen enough to give me a 'sweet eye' at the restaurant as I take his order. I ignore him and continue to write. Arrogant and show-self, he repeat the gesture when I serve him a beer, a wink with the left eye which he hold for a few seconds in case I miss it the first time.

'Study the menu carefully,' I instruct the braggart when I

return with his pig tail soup, 'look on it and tell me if you see my name on it. Show me where it mention Lorna Toney.'

No wonder the pang-belly captain now patronising a new restaurant in Walliabou.

Basil Lincoln totally different, I tell my mother when I recover from the ordeal, he was no ordinary man, he was from a higher sphere. It wasn't my fault, I explain to her, my conscience clear. For I didn't weaken: sometimes a woman is simply a victim of circumstances.

Something about the scream that Friday afternoon tell me at once that the culprit wasn't in real danger. If was a warning to an attacker, he well and truly fail. As I cross the bridge to the bus stop, the gesticulations suggest a man who wish to draw attention to himself, not one fearing for his life.

The man, Douglas Texeira, was in his late fifties. His black face seem too narrow for his heavy body, and his thick black hair explode on his head like he his own barber for too long. Shirtless, his skin grey and black, a string holding up his scruffy brown trousers, he was yelling at an invisible enemy hiding above the bus stop.

'Noah Francis,' he was calling out, 'you old coward, you wretch, why you don't come out the grass? Come out in the open where the sun can see your face!'

Three others witnessing this spectacle at the time: an old woman sitting in the middle of the bridge, the front of her skirt double-wrapped between her bony legs in the way of old women; a middle-age man on a grey donkey three sizes too small for someone of his bulk; and a child holding a bearded goat by a rope. Glad of an excuse not to rush home that evening, I linger with the others. I had to see Noah Francis. A man who choose to hide in the face of insults had to be worth at least a glance. So, having nothing better to do, I stay so I could to tell Debbie in my next letter how her village get 'bright'!

The screaming turn to jeering, accusations to taunts.

'Only a coward would poison a river in the dead of night. Come out Noah: unless you afraid to show your ugly face!'

No Noah Francis.

'I know you're in there Noah, you dirty night-worker.'

Still no Noah Francis.

Curiosity can only last so long. It occur to me after a while that perhaps no one actually in the grass. Like those leather-skin old men who spend their day thinking up childish pranks, Douglas probably playing a game with himself and inadvertently draw us into it. The young have their dreams, the old have to find a way to spend their decline. By now, though, a score or so of us loitering and hoping for some action for our trouble on a hot March afternoon.

A moment later, when it seem we wasting our time, Noah Francis slide down the bank, arms and legs spiralling as though someone hoof him from his hiding place. The entrance so theatrical, it make me think the two men about to perform some small drama for our afternoon pleasure.

We attentive now. What Noah going to do? How he going to react to the accusations? Under the hot sun we watch and wait. Noah drag himself to his feet and begin to brush his clothes. Dust rising with each desperate blow to his body, he resemble a man beating himself up. A little taller than Douglas, with a square face and short, grey, curly hair, he remind me of a child who forget to rinse the soap out of his hair. His blue shirt stained with mud, I watch him approach Douglas. A few metres away, he stop suddenly.

We wait. Ten seconds seem like an hour. A car drive by, the goat chew its rope like is some tough razor grass. Noah take a pace forward, Douglas stand firm.

Another long wait, the two men facing each other in the middle of the road by the wooden bus shelter.

'You going to pay for this, you know that, don't you?' Noah eventually end the silence.

'Who going to make me?'

'Me: me Noah Francis. You think you can go around insulting people, besmirching their character and good name and get away with it?'

'What good name? Since when poisoners have good name?'

'Poisoner? Who you calling poisoner?'

'You nuh!'

'Well I never poison a living soul.'

'You pour weedkiller into the river where people wash and fetch drinking water. Is only by God's grace no one get hurt.'

'I never set out to hurt anybody. The gramaxone stun the fish for half an hour so we can catch them: everyone know that.'

'Yes, but you could have killed the children who drink from the river.'

'I wasn't trying to injure, was the fish I was after: you deaf or what?'

'They outlaw that practice long ago, you know full well.'

'I didn't know.'

'You should, you're old enough. Ignorance is no excuse.'

Hands akimbo, Noah now move another step closer to Douglas, nostrils flaring, chest heaving, as if being called ignorant was the final straw.

'Douglas Texeira,' he warn, 'I giving you the chance to apologise. Take that chance or face the consequences!'

'If anyone need to apologise is you!' Douglas stand firm.

'Apologise!'

'Make me!'

'Say you're sorry!'

'Not to a man who have no consideration for others.'

Widening the country roads in SVG bring many benefits. For passengers and for businesses. Van-men profit too, but at the expense of common sense and regard for the law and the people they ferry. As we wait to see how Douglas and Noah going to resolve their dispute, two vans appear from the direction of Sans Souci. The roar of the engines mean just one thing. I shake my head sadly: why the police don't do their work? How many near-misses must it take before drivers realise the danger of overtaking round a bend?

As the drivers fight to avert a collision the screeching of the brakes cause the crowd to panic. The child drop the rope and holler, out of the corner of my left eye I glance the old woman on the bridge scramble to her feet to run for safety. That was the last thing I see clearly. Everything after was a blur.

People scatter in all directions, shouting and begging for their life. An arm ram into my chest, someone elbow me in the stomach. A clench fist in my left side throw me off balance, as I try to scamper, a leg trap mine. I fall backwards, slowly, so slowly it feel like I was ejected from my body. I witness my body trajectory from the outside, floating, falling, then crashing, the back of my head smashing against the stony ground.

Petra Ashby, a banana farmer from Spring Village, own two cars. The Honda smooth and reliable, she forever welding the other. Preparing the old Toyota for hire, each minute of spare time find her under the vehicle, sparks scattering in trails of blue, orange and white. When I land on the ground, the sensation was of a hammer blow to the back of my head. The violent crack release a fleet of those sparks, millions of the them, red, blue, orange, crackling, and hissing.

Trapped in my head, the sparks collide, rebound, scatter, the noise they make so deafening, like they going to rip off my head. I squeeze my eyes tight. I cover my ears to block out the noise. An electric current course round and round my head, threatening to short-circuit my brain. I was going to die, I was sure of it, death was just round the corner.

I scream. I hear my voice clearly, see myself separated from my body.

'Mommy, Daddy,' I shout, 'help me, please. I'm going to die!'

My head throbbing, my body in tremors, I yell with all my might.

'Help me, please, anybody! Debbie, come home now, come and save me!'

Eventually, with a splitting headache, I give up. Was obvious no one going to come to my aid. Lorna girl, a soft female voice whisper to me from a distance, you going to die at nineteen, you know. Your head smash. All your mother's hopes for you, you poor wretch, I really sorry for you.

A crazy vision of my mother reach me. She giving me a

public whipping, each whack of her favourite guava whip reverberating in the air.

'How could you die, you foolish girl, you just turn nineteen?'

Swish.

'How dare you die in such a stupid way, falling over by the roadside!'

Swish.

'You have to die grand, in a proper accident, from disease or old age: what's the matter with you, Lorna girl, eh?'

Swish.

Someone carry my injured body home, to this day I still don't know who responsible. And miraculously, the vans regain control, so that apart from a few scratches and bruises, people quickly forget the incident. In bed that night, light-headed and weak, I feel battered and tender. I want to get up but groggy like a newborn calf. Every part of my body ache. The hissing stop but, occasionally, a spark dart from one corner of my head and ping against the other. It hurt to lie on my back, my side and stomach even more tender. The only option was to try to sleep away the pain.

'About twenty,' I hear a soft female voice whisper while I dozing off. 'No more than twenty-one.'

I force to open my eyes. But locating the direction of the voice difficult. The weight of my head restrict my movement so I was obliged to search the room with my eyes. In the dim light I eventually discover the source, an elegant woman in her late-forties sitting at my dressing table. Legs crossed, left hand stroking her chin, she scribbling away in a notebook, a slight frown on her beautiful, high forehead. She wearing a loose-fitting turquoise trouser suit with wide lapels, and flat, black shoes. Her hair, in hundreds of fine plaits, bunched and tied stylishly at the back of her head.

'Yes, twenty, Mr Lincoln,' she resume the exchange with an invisible presence. 'Good-looking girl, five-five, nice thick black hair. Severe concussion, some kind of accident. I just arrive. Mount Greenan. St Vincent and the Grenadines, SVG.'

In my delicate state it take a while to realise that I was the subject of her conversation. Help at last, I say to myself, thank goodness!

I whisper, 'You a nurse?'

The woman pause, study a page, and transfer some information to a writing pad. If she could hear me, she give no sign.

'Who you talking to?' I ask. 'How you get into my room?'

Deep in concentration, she don't look up from her writing.

'My head,' I explain to her, 'please help me.'

My voice sound thin, like the bleating of a ram in the midday sun. If she hear me, it don't register.

'A civil servant of some kind, I believe,' she say in a pretty voice, stressing each word, without taking her eyes from the book. 'Mr Lincoln, it's bad, you will have to come yourself. She's definitely one for you.'

The voice fade. Silence control the room again. In the darkness I drift off. When I next look to my left the chair empty, the books gone. The affronted woman posing as nurse, how dare she come into my room! Her trouser suit just like mine, I just hope my clothes still in the wardrobe!

As I searching the room for the intruder, suddenly, from

nowhere, a palm gently lock onto my forehead. I let out a yelp from the shock. The fingers delicate but strong. Such a gentle and healing grip, who was it? When he remove his hand I make out the figure of a man standing over me. He in his thirties, handsome, with a full shapely nose and a thin, black moustache at the base of the top lip. His black skin soft, without a single blotch. So I wasn't seeing things, there was a nurse after all! Only now she turn into a man!

'My head,' I whisper to the man, 'do something. Please fix my head.'

In his face I see intense concentration, purpose, a desire to get on with his task. Too weak to repeat the questions I put to the woman, or to ask the hundred questions in my mind, I watch and wait.

He relax his grip, step back, approach again, and carefully place both index fingers on my temples. Applying a slight pressure, describing small circles with his fingers, he bring his face to within an inch of mine, his soft black eyes looking directly past me. His breath as hot as mine shallow. A cinnamon scent hover about him. I love cinnamon, the aroma lift my spirits, I feel better already.

'Hmmm,' he whisper, like a doctor faced with a puzzling ailment, 'hmmm.'

Drawing his head away from mine, the thumb and index fingers of his left hand come together to massage my forehead, light horizontal strokes meeting in the middle. Such precision and deftness: the pain lessen, I feel it seeping away. Silently I thank him: at least *he* recognise my needs, not like that useless nurse who probably empty my wardrobe before she scarper!

Ever so gently he run an index finger from my forehead down my nose. That touch! So light, so knowing! But when it stop it temporarily block my nostrils. Reacting instinctively, I try to grab it to shove it away. The man too swift, I end up with a handful of air. Like two children playing a game, the finger reappear on my lips, grazing them suggestively.

Back and forth, in a faint trail of cinnamon, he continue to stroke them, parting and closing my lips with his slow, fiery fingers. When his finger remain on the threshold of my mouth I know this was no nurse! No medical treatment in my experience involve this charade of fingers. I bite as hard as I could, sinking my teeth into the skin, tearing at the joints and crushing the bones. I crunch with all my strength, taste the bony finger trapped in the vice of my teeth.

'Take that you damn trickster!' I bellow. 'Get your nasty finger out of my blasted mouth!'

The man don't flinch. Not a trace of feeling in his face. He make me feel like a tiny hummingbird trying to carve a nest in the trunk of a cedar tree with its beak.

'Hmmm,' he say again, withdrawing the finger and taking a pace away from the bed, 'poor girl.'

On the right side of the room as you enter, near the door, is my dressing table. He walk slowly to it, sit, and start to consult a large volume lying there. Not one of my books I know for sure, for my collection is old paperbacks and withdrawn library stock. The volume he perusing have the dimensions of a world atlas, dense so till. A medical book, I assume.

My spirit rise. For somewhere in it there had to be a recommendation for a glass of water for a patient with a high fever. But I hope in vain. For when, some minutes later he find the correct page, he return to the bed empty-handed and stand directly over me, arms primed at his side, like a weightlifter preparing for a hoist.

'She's bad,' he say to himself, with the same urgent voice as the woman, yet strangely detached. 'She's bad for truth, is going to be awkward.'

As he confess this he look me over, exploring each region of my body with an easy eye. In my fragile state, I didn't care for the look. It remind me of the LIAT pilot. It make me recall also a singer at the restaurant who give me a lift home one evening and demand a kiss as payment for the ride and the song he hastily compose for me on the journey. This man look is direct, the eyes locked on mine. But, as I blink I swear I can feel him take in my entire body. Nurse or fraud, his eyes piercing and full of intent. I want healing, he seem like he want to inflict fresh wounds. Too weak to protest, I pretend I was asleep.

I feel hot fingertips drawing circles about my navel and hear a song in a language I don't understand. Sensitive to his soothing touch, I could feel myself becoming slightly aroused.

> *Tob. Eam. Ano. Ft. His. Wor. Ld.*
> *Su. Cha. Pret. Ty. Bl. Ackg. Irl.*
> *Th. Ewo. Rld. Hasn. Oth. Ingsw. eet. Er.*
> *Tha. Nap. Rett. Ybla. Ckgi. Rl.*

He sing the verse three times, softly, tenderly, not to me, but to my picture on the wall directly above the bed. His fingers gently massaging my lower stomach, his voice contain regret, confusion, desperation, attending to me seem distressingly painful for him, a curse, a sentence.

His voice so delightfully pure, I frighten I might yield. Crisp and melodious, it rise and dip with the oneness of a Baptist choir. I pray to remain strong, but I fear that any minute I might lose the battle to this man with the purity of a bird now that I could understand one of the verses.

> *To be a man of this world.*
> *Such a pretty black girl*
> *Earth has nothing sweeter*
> *Than a pretty black girl*

It feel so good, the song, the fingers, the tingling in my body, the pain melting away, but his fingertips igniting a slow charge within me. Stop the song, I beg him, please, no more, it destroying me. I have to close my eyes as he describe clockwise circles about my navel, gently kneading my stomach and making me quiver. Stop, I whisper, stop, please. No more damage, just make me better. Is that too much to ask?

As the song trail off the fingers get busy again. They drift upwards from my navel and pause between my breasts. Ashamed my body would acquiesce and begin to tingle again, I dare not open my eyes.

'Don't Mister,' I whisper, 'please don't. I'm sick, I'm not well. Please, I beg you.'

The fingers resume their journey after a brief pause. Up to the chin, lips and nose they saunter, calming and gentle, burning yet cool.

I feel tranquil now. A vision of the flat blue-green sea in Bequia drift into my mind. The soothing fingers return me to the state before the violent eruptions in my head. This man, the doctor, so good, what payment he expecting, what is his currency?

Swack! A bony palm crash into my left jaw. Swack! The doctor slap me again, this time with the back of his hand. Swack! Swack! Swack!

The sparks reignite in my head and set my head ringing. I yell, bawl out, summon all the reserves from my lungs and beg, 'No! Stop it nurse, don't hurt me doctor! I'm a sick girl, I'm dying. What did I do wrong?'

Swack! Swack! Swack! was the response, left and right. My jaw feel raw, I could taste warm blood where my teeth pierce the lining of my mouth.

He bring his face close to mine, so close I could almost taste the cinnamon on his breath. I ease my head back into the pillow but keep my eyes on him. His tiny eyes deep in their sockets but wild, penetrating and vicious. I can't afford to blink, I mustn't blink. I stare at him and he stare back. I concentrate, keep his entire face before my eyes, I mustn't lose him. My eyes still fixed on him, I feel like the lobe of my left ear on fire.

'Ahhhhhhhhhhhhhhhhh!' I bawl out. 'My ears, my ears! No, please, no! Please Mister, no more!'

Sinking his teeth deeper and deeper until my ear lose feeling, the beast seem determined to murder me! It hurt. The bite hotter than a needle dipped in a flame, the pain worse than a nail through your middle toe. Tears streaming down my face, I plead soft, I cry out in pain. I kick and punch with all the strength I could call on, I try to scratch his face. This was no nurse or doctor. It was Basil Lincoln himself!

'You hurting me, Mr Lincoln,' I whimper, begging to deter another attack, 'you're hurting me! Please don't hurt me any more. Whatever you want, do.'

I groan with pain. It hurt so much I didn't care if I die now. My ear ablaze like someone take a match to it, I sniff the air for the smell of burning flesh. As I sob and tremble I feel a warm hand on my forehead massaging my eyebrows and the other caressing my ear lobes as if to atone for the violence of the assault. Soft and gentle again, they extract the heat from my head and the sting from my ears.

Now that I recognise my tormentor my mother's warning make sense. More powerful than any living man, Basil Lincoln is truly one of the most vicious beings in the universe. And the most difficult to read. He have a pact with hell and the devil, yet he frequently spare sinners. Capable of wrecking families, carnal, brutal, how come he so gentle now again?

Caribbean folklore awash with strange creatures. On the page they safe, but for some people they in our midst day and night, they are a vital part of our lives. A rounce, a dog ten feet tall with enormous ears that sweep the ground, so terrify Medford Lockhart from Gomea as he strolling home at three o'clock in the morning that he give up his sweetheart, Vanessa Bute, from Cane Garden the following day. In broad daylight, as her parents preparing dinner, a creature lure away a five-year old girl from Enhams, never to be seen again. A hauntingly beautiful La Diablesse lift up her dress to reveal her cow hoof at the climax of a hot dance, jumbies avoiding the rain, blinding Jack Lanterns, the terrible power of a dark night!

Truth or fiction, above these creatures, stands Basil Lincoln. A man on Tuesday, a tiger the following day, pouncing on a victim, suffocating it, driving out life, he decide, you accept. Loving and caring in the morning, in the evening a bone-crushing haughty lion skilfully camouflaged in the bush, that is him also. Brute strength is the weapon of the lion and tiger, their appearance petrify. Imagine the terror on the face of Jemuel Goliath from Fairview who lift the lid of a bowl of fried breadfruit and discover a red snake winking at him! Or the wailing when Leola Ryan from Golden Grove discover a baby cobra dancing at the bottom of a steaming cup of coffee!

A master of disguise, that Basil Lincoln, different forms, same catastrophic result. The lion and tiger, a snap of the neck, the shudder of the heart, gone. But the Basil Lincoln who steal into my room mix surprise and cunning. Torture and pleasure seem like his weapons for me. Cruel, sadistic, anyone so dedicated to their work?

Now that I was in his grip I begin to wonder about my destiny. How was he going to decide whether I live or die? How to sway him? Survivors could recall only snippets of his method. Suspended between earth and hell, who could blame them? An elderly priest remember Basil Lincoln doing a pretty dance, a businesswoman who offer him a million-dollar bribe was spared: with her right arm fracture. For each victim he reprieve he adopt a different personality.

But at the end of his visit one thing for certain: you left with life, or condemned to eternal silence. And he alone possess the formula for that decision!

Since the nurse request him my situation had to be critical. Crossing the Atlantic Ocean and Caribbean Sea in an instant, Basil Lincoln was perpetually busy, rest and sleep beneath him, his work - death - was his life. Where his assistants falter, like the dibby-dibby nurse, Basil Lincoln was decisive. When he left me tonight I would be for this world, or condemned to a cold, bleak universe for a billion years.

I begin to pray, prayer was all I had in me.

'Please, Mr Lincoln, please don't take me. I am only nineteen, I am too young to go. I work hard and I don't steal from my employers. I'm not one of those modern girls who curse their parents and swear like they drag up. Spare me, I beg you, don't break my mother's heart. If you leave me on this side of the world I promise I will be good to my children and faithful to my husband. I've never had sex, I would like to travel on a 747. Spare me so I could see West Indies play good Test cricket again. I never leave SVG, I hear Cuba nice, India and Norway waiting for me to visit. Don't take me, Mr Lincoln, please. I'm not callous enough to ask you to take someone else in my place, but please, please, spare me. For my father's sake, for *my* sake.'

Eyes closed, I continue my desperate request. A million times I'm sure he hear these whimpers, but I had to plead, beg, do anything to stay in this world. But if he could hear my petition he give no sign. Emotion alien to him, it seem. Presently, I feel his finger carving, on my forehead, the words of the song.

> *To be a man of this world.*
> *Such a pretty Caribbean girl*
> *Earth has nothing finer*
> *Than a pretty Caribbean girl*

Returning to my temples, like a healer, he place his fingers there and chant the words this time slowly, his eyes closed as if he make his decision and ashamed to look me in the face.

A magician, a spirit, Basil Lincoln was the same cocoa-seed-black complexion of my uncle Mandrake. As he work I notice his soft, black hair and bony arms. His black face lined with Caribbean experience. Dressed in a grey cotton shirt and simple black trousers, if you add a pen to his breast pocket, he could pass for a tailor on the way to Kingstown to pay his land tax, or a man out to buy a black silk shirt for a dance. The man who hold my life in his hands as ordinary as my father.

When the chant end, he abandon the forehead and place his finger between my lips again. I sense he testing me and I don't know the correct response. Basil Lincoln is a man of games, I realise. Like he know me, but can't figure me out totally. To save myself I decide to trust my instincts. I have to play it as I see it. So I don't bite this time. Instead I close my eyes and resume my prayers.

'Please Basil Lincoln, don't let me die. Think of my mother, think of my father. You will have two more souls to take if you give me up. Please let me see Debbie qualify as a doctor.'

He withdraw his finger, casually, giving no sign of relief or displeasure. A moment later I feel my body being slowly rotated. By what means I still don't know to this day. From my back onto my stomach, some magical force turn me so that I end up with my face buried in the pillows. By shifting my head to the right I could see him standing looking me over. From the sway of my breasts as my body turn I realise I was in my underwear. Like a stupid schoolgirl I cover my eyes with my hands to hide my semi-nakedness.

'Please Mr Lincoln,' I pray, my voice muffled by the pillow, 'please don't take me, not now, not when I'm so young. I'm still on zero. Let me sleep with a man, let me taste the pain of childbirth. The librarian leaving for England next Friday, Clare Valley need someone to look after the place. Let me live, and I promise to live good.'

I feel his hands on the scar on the back of my head, comforting, healing. The raw smell of my blood-stained hair waft past my nostrils. A moment later my body return to its original position, rotating again, slowly, under the authority of the same invisible hand. I don't try to cover myself this time. I'm not ashamed of my body, I'm no longer afraid. Arms rigid at the side, my eyes open, fully conscious now, I can feel the blood spurting in my veins again. Basil Lincoln stare at me and I look him in the eye to let him know that, now, I could see him clearly.

He acknowledge my conscious state with a shallow nod, turn, and sit at the bottom of the bed. An enormous book open there. Again it not mine. From its brown jacket I could make out the title, *Caribbean Populations,* a favourite at the library. The book magically and obligingly open itself somewhere past the middle. His right index finger move slowly across the page. I watch him transfer some information to his notebook. Hesitating for an instant, his pen suspended in mid-air, he glance over at me. Then, the pen dancing with the speed and fury of his writing, he begin some complex calculations.

When these over, he ease himself up from the bed. The book close itself with a soft thud as he begin the final journey.

I don't flinch. I show neither fear nor anxiety. He make his decision, I prepared for it. Basil Lincoln approach me, slowly, and cast his sad black eyes over me. The room dark now, night finally replacing evening. The cinnamon smell appear again.

Without uttering a word he offer his left hand. But wasn't for a final reconciliatory handshake. Instead he calmly place the index finger between my lips again. I don't care now. If I have to go, I would leave my mark on him. He would suffer too, if he have it in him to feel pain! Some of my strength already return, he would know how I feel about him.

I don't wait. I bite as hard as I could. I take his finger to the back of my mouth and tear into them with my molars. Then, drawing strength from some source deep within my body, I sit up, punch and kick him in the stomach.

'Take that,' I tell him, 'you dirty, nasty, filthy, half-a-man, you take that! If you carry me away, my father will make you pay. You do anything to me and he will find you and destroy you. You useless half-a-man, you can only tease! You're not a real man. I am here half-naked and you can't do a thing. Two, three, four hours and you can't get further than staring and touching and singing! Now do what you want. I'm not afraid to die, Lorna Toney not afraid of you!'

With calculated slowness, Basil Lincoln extricate his finger from my mouth. I didn't hurt him, but I don't care. He tuck his shirt into his trousers and smile. A wry smile.

'Goodbye, Lorna Toney,' he say, acknowledging me directly for the first time. 'Goodbye.'

I swear I see sadness in his face, as if the evening drain him, as if he detest the nature of his work.

I close my eyes and say a silent prayer for my mother and father and for Debbie, and wish them goodbye. Like a woman at the guillotine I close my eyes and await my fate. Nineteen years too short for a life, I tell myself, but others have to satisfy with less. The world unfair, unjust, but high or low, you have to satisfy with your numbers.

'Electric shock?' I hear him respond to an invisible presence. 'Don't tell me, Grenada, right? When those people going to learn to respect electricity?'

He look at me and smile again and, in an instant, he was gone. When I catch myself daylight was streaming through the window.

the hole

A July Saturday, the boys at the card game by the rickety bamboo shed adjoining Simoney's shop. Bundle, Vronin, Mothers and Tonic playing rummy, dollar a game. Sun hot to burn down the country, the afternoon calling out for a dip in the sea. But Lionel prefer to remain with the boys. Two miles to the beach is two miles too far. Bedsides, he waiting for the opportunity to win back his twenty.

For all his twenty-six years Lionel Scrubbs live in Gomea. Flanked by sleepy Fairview and explosive Three Acres, Gomea sit peacefully in the interior of the island. A mist hover menacingly above the village. The roads spring and, as in South Rivers, the sight of a land crab scurrying for the bushes in the midday sun won't interrupt a game of hopscotch. Standing in the shade waiting another turn at cards, Lionel hear a voice whisper his name. When he turn to his left, he find Alban Dogandal.

'Hey, Alban,' Lionel greet him, 'you back?'

'Yes man,' Alban reply, his voice barely a whisper.

'Since when?' Lionel ask.

'Yesterday.'

'Good trip?'

'You could call it that.'

'Catch plenty fish?' Lionel enjoy using the code he hear Alban use to deter those who want to delve too deep into his business.

'Mullets and sprats.'

'Small ones then?'

'Not every day man can catch tuna. How things in the village?'

'Quiet.'

'You winning?'

'What you think?'

'Another losing streak, eh?'

'Is only a dollar game,' Lionel go on the defensive. 'No big thing.'

'Time you move up to a higher division,' Alban suggest. 'You play too low.'

'How you mean?'

'Come with me and I will tell you.'

'Where?'

'Just come nuh man: stop breaking old style like a bride.'

'But the game just getting sweet!'

'Rummy can wait: come talk business.'

Muscular, with long powerful arms, Alban twenty-five. A former choirboy with a disarming smile, lately he develop a menacing streak. Not that he ever threaten anyone. Was his sneer that unsettle, and his silence. Once joyful and mischievous, he rarely talk now. A shallow nod and a grudging smile seem all he could spare. He always appear preoccupied. The young man who used to organise the annual race round the village now a bored spectator at all events. Locked in his house for days, he lose interest in everything and everyone in Gomea.

Short and plump and gentle, Lionel renown for his strength. Wherever serious lifting call for, only one man to call. Everyone love him. Slow and heavy, he get a genuine welcome in Gomea, Buccament and nearby Simon. Famous for his appetite, he like to boast that wherever he stop a large bowl of food put before him within ten minutes. The new Alban, disappearing for days, returning suddenly then stealing away again, make people feel uncomfortable. Lionel the only one who blind to the complete transformation.

Alban's 'errand boy', his 'tamboo-bamboo': Lionel count the Alban others fear as a friend. Smoking or drinking, he content to join him watching the children playing cricket or 'Thief' in the road. No matter Alban didn't say much, Lionel have talk for them both, he tell those who warn him. Whenever Alban fancy an expensive brand of cigarettes or a foreign rum, Lionel only too willing to run to the shop. The short trip for flour, rice or smoked herring for a late night cook net him ten dollars, unloading coconuts from a Jeep, a handy thirty.

'Hold a twenty': three times in the past month Alban press a stiff red note into his palm in the dusk of early evening and whisper, 'Come and check me later'. Curious to find out what 'business' Alban have for him this time, Lionel abandon the card game and duly follow him to his house.

Squatting on nine tall concrete pillars, Alban's house deceptively modest. It consist of a 'parlour' and two bedrooms with the windows permanently shut. The brightest day seem like a dark rainy evening within it. Alban offer Lionel some bread and cheese and, to wash these down, a large glass of sweet lime juice the way he know Lionel like it. Then, from the parlour he lead Lionel to the kitchen, a large wooden structure to the south of the house.

The thick wooden door of the kitchen secured with two solid metal locks. Lionel wait patiently while Alban wrestle with the locks, sucking his teeth in frustration and swearing under his breath. A gentle kick, a shove with the shoulder, and it eventually budge. When they enter Lionel realise it wasn't a kitchen at all, but a store of some kind.

Sacks cover the floor, some lying horizontally, others upright. Somewhere between twenty and thirty cardboard boxes carefully stacked in a corner. Dumbstruck at this discovery, Lionel let out a loud gasp.

'What inside the sacks,' he ask innocently, 'you running a shop or something?'

'Plums,' Alban reply in a low monotonic voice, a warning which don't register with Lionel.

Lionel lift the bag closest to him as though to test Alban's statement.

'But this bag heavy like hell!' he say to Alban, holding the bag up to his chest.

'Exactly,' Alban say, hoping Lionel would get the message, 'it full of plums.'

'And the others?'

'Plums.'

'Every single one?'

'Plums.'

'The boxes?'

'Plums.'

'Oh I see,' Lionel finally get his warning, 'you not going to tell me?'

'Is best you don't know: if you don't know you can't lie.'

'Lie about what?'

'Lionel,' Alban explain, like a teacher to a pupil, 'the reason I ask you here is because we going on trip. We have to take the sacks somewhere.'

'Where?'

'Don't ask that question.'

'Far?'

'Couple of miles.'

'But me and you can't carry all of them,' Lionel point out the obvious.

'Don't worry: is just one bag each today, the rest can wait.'

'I taking this one,' Lionel joke, selecting the closest bag, 'it light, somebody forget to load it up with plums.'

Alban put a restraining hand on Lionel shoulder. 'Your bag the one in the middle, let me get it for you.'

'But all the bags look the same!' Lionel protest.

'You could say that. But this one need careful handling.' Alban fetch the sack for Lionel. 'It need a man with strength and stamina.'

Alban give him a half-smile, Lionel accept the sack and, lifting it to his chest, he smile back at Alban. For though the sack top-heavy, the weight no more than a well-fed child.

'Now, listen to me, Lionel,' Alban say, his voice soft but loaded. 'Understand what I telling you. We carrying the bags to the mountains, we going to spend a couple of days. Three hundred dollars in it for you if things go well, if you prove you can keep quiet and spend your money discreet, you can make hundreds, enough to set you up.'

'Who me?' Lionel ask, picturing himself counting out a thick wad of notes.

'Yes you.'

'Three hundred EC dollars?'

'More if you prove you can perform.'

'Then what we waiting for?' Lionel ask as he grab his bag, 'let's go nuh.'

The sea might not have one, but each village has a back door. From the humblest to the proudest, in every country on this earth. A narrow bushy track, a rocky downhill path, a short cut behind some forbidding tree that allow the villager in a tight spot to slip away, a village recognise the duty to protect its own.

Shielded by rows of coconut trees, down Eustace Hill Alban and Lionel trod a few minutes later. Bags on their shoulders, no one witness their departure. On the flat between the fat pork trees and sharp razor grass, Lionel turn to look back at Gomea with the wistful gaze of a man saying goodbye to a lover. His feet landing in the holes where the soft black sand give way, staying upright using all his dexterity, he sense that this journey going to mark a turning point in his life.

Lionel know the area well, so he quickly he realise Alban not taking the concrete track to the mountains. Instead, through dense banana fields, up steep banks of yam vines they trek, silent and out of sight. Clearing a path through the bush with their free hand, brushing away overhanging branches, climbing over huge boulders and sharp rocks, Lionel dying to ask why they avoiding the level road half a mile away. Sweat trickling down his chest and bare arms, the brisk pace Alban setting already proving difficult for him but, from Alban's grim determination, he know better than to ask or complain.

Through the gaps in the fragrant cocoa trees to the left of the river, he see, in the distance, the mango trees at Bonhomme and the spiky gru-gru trees. The child in him wish he could wander over, chop a green branch, and return to the village to share the prized gru-gru with his friends. On the morning breeze, above the murmur of the river, he hear voices from the road. At last, as the river straighten out between the banana field and nutmeg trees at Hope Stretch, Alban grunt for them to rest.

Allowing the bag to roll gently off his shoulder and down his right hand, Lionel catch it before it reach the ground. He stand it upright then, glad of the rest, he lower himself onto a nearby stone, huffing and panting like a man twice his age.

As he hunch over to catch his breath, he could make out the workers in the arrowroot field to his left, tiny figures, silhouettes of black in the green landscape. Two days earlier, he remind himself, was him in that very field, was Lionel Scrubbs toiling under the hot sun. To their right, his machete glinting in the sun, he spy Melvin Hippolyte, almost seventy, tidying his bananas, the giant leaves floating slowly to the ground. No way, he promise himself, no way he going to labour like that beyond sixty. By hook or by crook, he determined to find an easier way to earn his living.

Because of the rocky terrain, few people venture deep in the mountains in this part of the island. Hunters of iguanas or manicou, or young boys in search of more exotic stripy lobsters, groupers, or eels. Lionel stare at the trees, tall and thick, with huge trunks, long beards and tangled-up roots. They enormous and strange, he feel like he in a foreign land. The concrete road give way to a muddy track and this, in turn, lead to a path of brown trodden grass. An hour from Hope Stretch, his back tight, his neck stiff, knees buckling, Lionel feel like a wreck.

'Not long now,' Alex say in his deep bass voice. 'The track end here. We going by the river now.'

Lionel's heart sink. The strongest man in the village, yet he feel like a real weakling. Sweating, gasping for breath, for a blasted three hundred dollars, look how he punishing himself! But what choice he have? Turn back now and let Alban laugh at him? Return to Gomea and have dog and cat call him salt? Not this Lionel. So he lumber on, his legs getting heavier and stiffer, every muscle in his body raw. Even if it kill him, he mutter to himself, he going to complete the journey.

Cold and numbing, the river never feel so uninviting Where it deep the cold burn his legs. Battling against the steady flow, he coax himself, recall all the loads he lift and all the praise he receive. As the tightening in his thigh muscles spread to his calves, feeling lame and useless, he have to draw on all his reserves to continue.

For a mile they battle, still in silence, Lionel praying for an end to the pain, Alban striding purposefully on. In the shallow, using all his strength he catch up, but soon he languishing again. Sweating like a pig, his legs frozen, Lionel clench his teeth and pray. Let me complete the journey, he ask silently, give me the strength to see it to the end. Through the stony sections of the river he waddle, the sack unsteady on his shoulder. Finally, without warning, without a landmark Lionel could detect, they leave the river and climb up a gentle embankment on the left.

There, before them, Lionel make out a huge area of flat ground at the base of a steep expanse of naked, brown earth. Two small wooden houses stand side by side, fifty yards apart, and in the 'yard', coconut branches stacked to form an enormous heap.

'Lionel, we reach,' Alban say unnecessarily.

He help Lionel to set down the load and Lionel exhale with an audible sigh of relief.

'You passed the test,' Alban congratulate him, 'you do very well. Some men turn back first time.'

'The journey tough,' Lionel admit, 'another corner in that blasted river, and that was me finished.'

'Nah, you stronger than that, Lionel,' Alban continue to butter him up. 'You always do what you have to. That is why I decide to take you on board.'

Hands flopping by his sides, Lionel lower himself wearily and gratefully onto a nearby stone. A few moments later, the door of the larger house open and a man step out. He about their age, Lionel guess, medium height, good-looking, with full shapely lips like a woman's, and a slender delicate neck. His short wavy hair part down the middle. Shirtless, he wearing khaki shorts with a yellow belt from which a small sword dangle.

'Captain,' Alban greet the man with a hug. 'The others back yet?'

Captain shake his head and glance at a watch on his left hand. 'Any time now,' he reply in a soft effeminate voice. 'The river a bit heavy from the rain.'

'Come,' Alban say to him, taking him by the left elbow, 'I have something special for you.'

Alban fetch Lionel's bag and invite Captain to test it. With the tip of the sword Captain prod the bag at the base, in the middle, and near the top. He undo the cord and take a long careful look. He grin, then a big smile come over his face.

'Good harvest man,' he say, taking Alban by the waist, 'ten more of these and we definitely ruling the town.'

Captain on one side, Alban on the other, they do a pretty little dance about the bag, then embrace again.

Lionel baffled. After the fuss in the kitchen, after Alban insist that all the bags the same, he end up carrying a 'special bag'! Alban dupe him, he suddenly realise, from now on he have to be on his guard. But what the bag contain to prompt such ceremony? Something going on, he say to himself, Alban trees bearing golden plums, he catching fish when other men run out of bait. He, Lionel, definitely need to watch out. But wet and exhausted, rest more urgent now than investigation. So when Alban indicate the small house to change and relax Lionel go gladly.

A house in appearance from the outside, the smaller building bare within. No furniture, some cotton sheets on the floor, nothing else. Not even a window. In the darkness Lionel peel off his trousers, and spread it on the floor beside him to dry. Within five minutes he fast asleep.

When he wake up was well after three o'clock. The July day hazy, with a slight drizzle, but stiflingly hot. He put on the damp trousers and make his way outside. In a corner of the yard, he find six men sitting on firestones next to a huge aluminium pot to the right of the smaller house. The moment he approach, one of the men pick up a calabash from the floor and serve him an enormous helping.

'Thanks fellas,' Lionel say, with a huge grin, 'you must could read my mind.'

The men nod in acknowledgement but, instead of the outburst of laughter he expect, they return directly to their food.

'Where you fellas from?' he ask, as he take his first spoonful.

As if he break some unwritten rule, the men stop eating, turn in unison and glare at him. The glare neither harsh nor timid. But it unsettle Lionel. It make him feel like a man late to church asking the order of service.

'What happen,' he ask, his confusion mounting, but trying to make light of it, 'you fellas can't speak, or you take some kind of oath?'

Their heads bowed, chewing quietly, Lionel get the answer. So, learning quickly, he, too, join the silence.

Not long after the meal over, Alban and Captain emerge from their house. Alban now sporting a red string vest and green shorts, Captain grey combat trousers and a tight purple shirt that reveal slender but shapely biceps. With an upward sweep of the right hand, but without a word, Captain signal to the men to remove the branches in the yard. Lionel push his empty calabash aside and watch intently.

The men drag the coconut palms, dry and green, from the pile and stack them neatly in a corner of the yard. In the light drizzle they work quickly and skilfully. Within five minutes, as the bottom layer peel away, they uncover a huge tarpaulin. Like soldiers awaiting the command to advance, the men turn to Alban and Alban look at Captain. Captain nod, and the men get the message. They remove the twelve stakes that secure the tarpaulin, then two of the men drew the tarpaulin to one side.

'Peas and rice!' Lionel emit an audible gasp. 'What the hell is that?'

A deep circular hole open before them like a gaping sore in the ground. Radios, tyres, crocus bags, car batteries, wooden boxes, crates of beer, an engine, bottles of rum and whisky, sacks of potatoes, tins of biscuits, wooden chairs, cardboard boxes, unopened sacks: Lionel stand open-mouthed, amazed. Fear grip him. He could feel his heart stuttering, he start to pant. What kind of business Alban and Captain mixed up in? he wonder. For a miserable three hundred dollars, what he get involved in?

Learning quickly, he keep the questions to himself. The novice in the group, he judge it better to observe and fall in line. So he stand back as two of the men begin to fill a large crocus bag. They take out boxes of cigarettes, bottles of beer and rum, kitchen towels, a car battery and tins of sardines, and pack them carefully. They then secure the bag with a strong rope. With an easy hoist the smaller of the two men lift the bag onto his left shoulder. His companion look in the direction of Alban and Captain for instructions.

Alban fetch Lionel's bag and address the smaller man. 'Chief, you going to Belvedere, don't forget. Colonel waiting at the boxing plant. Look after this cargo with your life.' Turning to the other he say, 'Private, Richmond for you: link up with Sarge by the rain tree at Belleisle Hill.'

The men set off, Captain and Alban return to their house, Lionel and the other men to the bare floor of the other.

For the next three days, with a mixture of fear, curiosity and anticipation, Lionel observe the comings and goings. Each morning new men with sacks arrive. Some stay the night, others head back for the river with a fresh bag, contact instructions, and an envelope Lionel assume to be their payment. No discussions, no questions. All 'operations' conduct with the minimum of words, the men like strangers, happy in their anonymity, cogs in this mountain activity.

Grown men, strapping, wiry or athletic, reduced to silence deep in the mountains! Was the most disconcerting thing Lionel ever witness. He totally baffled. Loud and vivacious in their village, he was sure, yet here, when gambling, eating or arm wrestling, they grunt like beasts and gesture like children!

None have a name, no one bother to enquire about your village or town! Your family or friends? Not the slightest interest. No way he going to live that life, he promise himself, not Lionel Scrubbs. Never letting up, the mountain animals chirping, squawking and hissing. No animal going to better Lionel Scrubbs, he tell himself, when the time right, his voice going to be well and truly heard!

In contrast, in what one of the men label the 'great house', constant argument raging. From the yard Lionel spy a wooden bed and two chairs, and every night Captain and Alban seem to be dismantling the furniture. The arguments might last an hour, sometimes a ferocious ten minutes. He hear threats to leave, he make out Alban promising to break Captain leg, their whimpering seem to him the reconciliation of lovers.

Through the arguments the men sleep calmly and without concern. Only a particularly violent incident could interrupt their card game. For however bitter the argument, when Alban and Captain emerged the following day, no one question their authority or ask the cause of their quarrels.

All this time the rain in the mountains getting more ferocious, especially in the evenings. From every angle the rain lashing the house, pounding it as though in a terrible rage. The river swell, driving the men to find even more arduous routes to and from the base. Drenched and weary, one of the new arrivals collapse from the journey through the river and muddy fields.

At night, the thunder drowning the arguments from the great house, Lionel sleep soundly, with sweet memories of his beloved Gomea. The children playing in the street without a care in the world, the men playing cards and drinking, the women smiling, discussing their hair in an impenetrable language: he miss them all, he pray for a safe return to the bosom of the village.

On the third day, without giving anything away, Alban instruct the five men in the house to dig a hole, 'fifteen feet deep and wide'. Captain expecting a special shipment, he explain, a new hole required, and urgently. A speedboat, a bearded man whisper, the moment Alban depart, Captain and Alban planning to branch out to St Lucia. 'Speedboat now,' the man add, 'helicopter next'.

The men dig. Four at a time, they fork, pick and shovel, ignorant of the mission, but loyal to their paymasters. Sweat pouring from their bodies, their hair and hands caked in mud, they stop only for a beer or cigarettes. Physical men, adventurers, fed up of card games, arm wrestling, reading tattered westerns and old newspapers, they grateful for the opportunity to work for their pay.

From time to time Alban or Captain come out to monitor their progress. Their quick return to the house Lionel and the other men take to indicate their satisfaction with their work. So they redouble their efforts. Like men possessed, they attack the brown-black earth, pounding, scooping and hurling in a smooth controlled motion, repeating the cycle, determined to prove their worth to themselves and to one other. Softened by the rain, the earth give. Six hours later, the hole completed, they return to the house to rest their aching bodies.

After their meal and a dip in the river to remove the mud and sweat, the others quickly nod off. But although tired, Lionel restless. What Alban and Captain planning? he wonder. What so important they have to work through the drizzle? As he sit on the floor wondering, thunder claps begin to rock the house. Rain pound it mercilessly. But thunder and rain didn't bother him. In the desolation of the mountains the thunder feel like an earthquake, but that would soon pass. Why Captain and Alban look so pleased with themselves, he ask himself repeatedly, what they up to?

Just after seven, the rain still hammering, the door to their house wrench open and, drenched and anxious, Alban and Captain race in.

'Landslide,' they both shout at the same time, 'landslide!'

The sleeping men shoot up.

'What?' they ask.

'Landslide,' the two repeat, 'landslide washing away the house!'

The five men scamper outside. There, behind the 'great house', they see a huge mass of earth where a section of the bank slip. A mountain of soft brown mud some thirty yards away from the house. The men shrug their shoulders and return to their tiny house. Like high winds and tropical storms, landslides a feature of the rainy season, they mumble, no point in worrying. Just as they settle down to a game of cards Captain cough for attention.

'Fellas,' he announce, 'we have a little problem.'

The men place their cards face down on the floor, fold their arms and listen.

'This house,' Captain continue, getting straight to the point, 'it too small for seven of us.'

'But you have your own house,' one of the men point out.

'What Captain mean,' Alban interject, 'what Captain trying to say, is that we going to swap houses for the night.'

'Why,' the man ask, 'what wrong with yours?'

'We can't run operations with the threat of another landslide,' Alban reply.

'The weak part of the bank already released,' Lionel explain, 'your house safe unless it rain for forty days and forty nights.'

'Me and Captain need our sleep so we can plan things properly,' Alban reply, in a soft voice that dare anyone to contradict him. 'Our customers have to get their supplies.'

'Is uproar if anybody go short,' Captain add, 'and if we don't get a good night's rest and the clients don't get their goods, you fellas don't get pay.'

'The loose earth already slide down,' Lionel repeat, 'and the terrace behind your house going to dissolve with the rain. No need to worry.'

'Lionel, I hear what you saying,' Alban answer, 'but Captain already make the decision: we swapping house tonight: you fellas have to take your belongings and shift!'

The men don't argue. Secretly, they relish the chance to stay in the 'great house'. To sleep on a bed, to sit upright on a proper chair, to play cards on a table, they could put up with that. Hardened, unafraid, men who trekked through the mountains alone at night, why bother about a little landslide? They gather their bundles and, in the driving rain, relocate without fuss.

The thunder persist. Like millions of nails from a gun, the raindrops drill into the sides and roof of the house. Through a lull, Lionel hear screaming and shouting and, after a while, a distant, soft moaning like a wounded animal pleading to be put out of its misery. He feel sorry for it but what could he do? Eventually, he creep onto the bigger bed, nudge one of the men onto his side, and soon fall asleep.

The next morning the rain and thunder relent. The air fresh and clear. The storm of the previous night seem like a distant memory. But the men in no hurry to go outside. For the great house contain not only two beds, a table and chairs, but a solid wooden wardrobe. Inside the wardrobe they find four cardboard boxes stacked on a trunk. One of the boxes contain bread, tarts, tins of sardines, smoked herring, biscuits, ham, cheese and beer, the other, clothes. The huge metal trunk locked. Using all his strength, Lionel prise away the lock.

'Peas and rice!' he exclaim, when he lift the lid, 'fellas, come and have a look at this.'

The men stand over the trunk, three of them mildly surprised, the other have the indifferent look of someone peering inside a simmering pot placed on the fire an hour earlier. In bundles of twenty and hundreds, the trunk stuffed with piles of EC dollars. Below these, layers of English pounds, French francs, pesetas, US dollars and other foreign currency.

'Peas and rice,' Lionel repeat, 'where they get all this money?'

'You don't know?' one of the men ask.

'No,' Lionel reply.

'Seriously, you don't know?' The man look at him incredulously.

Lionel spit in the palm of his left hand and draw a cross to swear he didn't.

'Then get out of this business before you get in too deep,' advise another. 'Get out *now*. Go back to your village, make back with your woman, or go home to your family. Get out before is too late.'

Still in a state of shock, Lionel close the trunk, and follow the men outside to prepare breakfast.

A trail of mud from the small house to the hole slightly surprise him. A trickle now, he realise that the small house suffer a landslide as well. The house intact but this slippage appear ten times more devastating than that behind the 'great house'. Following the trail, the men go directly to the hole.

There, up to the waist in mud, their eyes bloodshot, they discover Alban and Captain.

'Where the hell you fellas been all this time?' Captain ask, the moment he see them. 'You know how long we down here?'

'All night we calling out, 'Alban was fuming, 'and none of you have the damned sense to come and get us out!'

'We hear the landslide coming, we run out the house, we fall and slip into the hole,' Captain explain. 'We scream and yell and, instead of helping, all of you sleeping like blasted children or as if you on honeymoon!'

Lionel stare at his friend, his face a brown, muddy mask. Trapped in mud, fists clenched, and full of rage, he imagine their desperate attempts to climb up the hole only to slip back, like crabs in a basket. Shirtless, weak from the effort of trying to escape, who was Captain to order anyone about?

'Pull you out,' Lionel ask, 'how we going to do that?'

'Get the blasted rope,' Alban scream with a venom Lionel never believe him capable of. 'Look in one of the boxes in the wardrobe: it have a tow rope in there, bring it!'

'Don't bother about the rope,' Captain holler, 'just lower some coconut branches: if two of you pull, you could get us out in a couple of minutes.'

The men look on, not knowing what to do. Accustomed to Captain and Alban making all the decisions, they stand there like they can't remember right from wrong. But Lionel know what to do.

'Don't bother with the coconut branches,' he say. And blocking the way of the man making for the great house he warn, 'Leave the rope in the trunk.'

Captain make another attempt to climb up the hole, grasping at the sides, growing weaker with each desperate attempt. Eventually he sink back, the mud sucking him to the middle.

'Fetch the blasted rope,' he order. 'Get it, or when I get out of this hole all of you in serious trouble! If any of you think you can hide, you making a big-big mistake!'

'Forget the rope,' Alban scream, 'just get a blasted branch and pass it down to me!'

He try to swim to the side but back to the centre of the vast abyss he slide, the mud sucking him like a powerful magnet.

'Help me, Lionel,' Alban try a different tact, 'get the rope and pull me out. It have a thousand dollars in the trunk: if you rescue me you can have the money.'

'A thousand dollars, did you say a thousand?' Lionel ask.

'Two thousand,' Alban reply, his desperation mounting, 'just get me out.'

'Two thousand? Only two thousand?'

'Two thousand from me, two thousand from Captain.'

'What about the rest?' Lionel ask.

'What rest?'

'The trunk full of money, Alban, we find the treasure trove.'

'However much you want you can have, money not a problem. You and the others just get me and Captain out of this hell, and quick: the sky darkening again: another shower and we finished!'

The men stand on the opposite bank to the trickle of mud watching the two pathetic souls. Their eyes! The terror in their eyes! Up to the waist in muddy water, in a hole twenty feet deep, desperate, men who deserved their fate.

Lionel know exactly what he have to do.

'It have any kerosene?' he ask.

Unsure what he have in mind, the men look at him.

'Kerosene,' Lionel order, 'get some kerosene!'

The men get him now. They know what he planning. They know what *they* have to do.

'It have a box of matches in the great house,' one of them point out.

'Good,' Lionel say. He turn to the men. 'Now, if you fellas

want money, go and help yourself. Take however much you want.'

The men stare at one another as Lionel take a seat on a stone. Then they turn and stare in the direction of the house. From the rim of the hole they turn their gaze to Captain and Alban. For a minute they remain like this, wrestling with their consciences. But no man move. Each man come to realise that his true worth could never be in easy dollars or pounds.

'Good,' Lionel say. 'Now, fetch the matches, and bring the clothes from the wardrobe.'

Recognition now dawn on the men. They could break the silence. They fetch the clothes and douse them in kerosene. Removing the tarpaulin, they light the clothes and lower them into the old hole stocked with goods. They add coconut branches, wood from the houses and the chairs and tables, stand back and watch. In minutes they hear the sweet song of fire and a series of tiny explosions.

'The trunk,' Lionel have a sudden thought. 'Fetch the trunk.'

Two of the men drag the trunk and place it by the edge of the hole. In the background they could hear the threats and swearing and promises to tear their limbs from their bodies.

'All of you going to pay for this,' Alban yell. 'Lionel, you first. You the ringleader. Don't think any of you getting away with this.'

Lionel don't even bother to listen. Doomed, Captain and Alban have no power now. The hole deep, more rain in the air, the elements would do their job.

'Empty the trunk,' Lionel order, 'empty it into the hole.'

Two of the men tip it over the edge and apply a match. They could hear the crisp notes crackle, they watch them wither and drift to the bottom.

'The houses,' one of the men say, 'what about the houses?'

'Burn them,' Lionel don't need to think twice, 'destroy both of them.'

The men pour kerosene throughout the houses, soak the sides, the roofs, and cover every square inch. They hurl kerosene-soaked branches and retreat quickly. After a short delay, explosions tear the houses apart. Deliciously red, the flames devour the buildings like a starved wood-eating monster.

When nothing remain but ashes, the men shake hands and introduce themselves. Melvyn Ambris from Belmont, Arnold Black from Riley, Noel Stephens from Overland, Ratty Goliath from Paul's Lot and Moses Sampson from Belmont, they find their voices again. The men don't bother to take a final look at Captain and Alban. They forge a new trail through the German Joe trees and return to their beloved villages and towns, and to their loving families.

p q r

The years we spend in school make or break us, they fund our dreams or fuel our nightmares. Trundling along, day after day, term after term, the rituals comfort or frustrate. If we are lucky, something appears, and our eyes are suddenly opened. Or someone. But we have to be ready.

Caroline Chatoyer was fifteen. A quiet girl, mad on sport, four years earlier, in the middle of winter, she had joined her parents in England. She missed the Caribbean, the sun and sea, and her friends. But, as a groom accepts the timid hand of his bride, she had grown to accept England as her home. She was daydreaming during her French lesson one afternoon when she heard her teacher's voice.

'Now, Caroline, what are we going to do with you?' Mr Rees asked wearily. 'Two years of French and what have you got to show for it?'

Mr Rees paused, bit a thoughtful lip, and then resumed

pacing the room. His was a slow trot, with small dainty steps like a well-trained pony. Staring intently at each face, he smiled encouragingly. Strict, but concerned for their welfare, he wasn't in the business of humiliating pupils.

'I'm sorry Mr Rees,' Caroline stammered, her head bowed, 'but I can't help it: I'm just no good at languages.'

The teacher stared sympathetically at her, like a father at a mischievous child.

'You need to practise, my dear, how many times have I told you? Practise! That's the only way to improve. A little less time on the sports field and a bit more on your lessons, then who knows what might happen?'

Mr Rees was thin, with a narrow, chalk-white face. Sporting a brown suit, he looked like a twenty-year old although, she guessed, he had to be approaching fifty. Caroline didn't fear him like others feared their teachers. Teacher or pupil, she was afraid of no one. He wanted the best for her and her classmates: she just wished she didn't disappoint him so often.

'I do try, Sir,' she replied, 'but it just doesn't sink in.'

'Well, just put in that *little* bit extra. Promise?'

'I will, Sir, I promise.'

'Good. Now, just to prove that you haven't lost it entirely, have a go at this in French: "I must work harder because I want to succeed."'

Taking her time, Caroline rehearsed the answer in her head, selecting from her fragments of French vocabulary.

'Je dois,' she began, 'je dois travailler parce que, parce que, parce que....'

'......A bit more work to do there,' Mr Rees smiled

encouragingly then moved on. 'But, thank you Caroline.'

Claremont was a comprehensive of 1200, a median school in a small town 30 miles west of London. Its mixed pupil population - Caribbean, Asian, English - made the treacherous two miles up Blue Hill on dark winter mornings as loosely integrated on the bus as they mixed at the school itself. Dull grey skirts and trousers, with matching jumpers and blazers, formed the uniform, allowing those who so wished to melt into glorious invisibility on foggy days.

And invisibility could have been the school's motto. For the Caribbean students in Caroline's year, invisibility and pointlessness. For few saw any real purpose in the automatic progression from form to form, the able and the idle receiving the identical reward.

Caroline shifted uneasily in her seat. She could feel a rush of heat to her face. She dared not look around, for her classmates in 4C could be merciless. They laughed at anything. Anyone who stumbled was fair game. Lauren Clarke, an English girl with greasy black hair, who always talked as though she was stuck on full volume, had teased Norman Morris so cruelly about his thinning hair that he had asked for a transfer, even though it meant demotion to 4F. Timid and shy, a bar of soap placed on her chair during a tutorial had driven Sally Alderslade to a rival school ten miles away.

Their language often matched their actions. Pushing open the door to the gym one autumn afternoon, Caroline overheard two 5B girls in conversation as they dressed after cross-country.

'Did you see Karen?' asked the first, a plump girl with fleshy pink thighs.

'Who, Karen Dodds?' replied the other, patting her soft hair into a rounder afro.

'Yes, *her*.'

'Why?'

'I hate her.'

'Why?'

'The saggy-pussy blonde witch, she only tried to come on to my boyfriend, didn't she!'

'Did she really? I told you she was a thief!'

Dressing in record time, Caroline had hurried to the track to practise.

The French expression on which she had stalled that afternoon, *Parce Que*, echoed in her head like a stuck record. Soon, she feared, she would be the talk of the school.

For wherever Caribbean students gather, nicknames swiftly and inevitably follow. Some fall off, but once a name sticks, it is virtually impossible to erase. Marva Tella, from Jamaica, her lips permanently puckered, was 'Kisssss', Gia Holder, with skinny black legs that shone from regular applications of Vaseline, 'Bajan Sparrow'. Chubby and wicked, Kevin Crichton, from St Kitts, who finished everyone else's dinner grinned approvingly when called 'Hoover'.

Blissfully unaware, some of the English students sported nicknames also. Elaine South, who in a desperate attempt to be black, twisted her brown hair into ugly, grainy plaits, was 'Bwack', Nigel Moon, who had grazed his throat during a metalwork lesson, 'Strangler'. So the black students must have fallen asleep that afternoon, Caroline assumed. Either that or, dreading being asked to translate a passage, they were trying to summon up all the French words they knew.

That Monday afternoon, feeling small, flimsy, worthless, Caroline decided to walk home after school. She needed time by herself. She wished to think over Mr Rees's words alone, without the distraction of the E 59 bus with its teenage passengers and joyriding pensioners.

Mr Rees was right, she was forced to admit, as she trekked through the woods at Blue Hill, she deserved his stinging words. There she was, fifteen, in her penultimate year, yet the idea of a career hadn't occurred to her. The procrastination had to end, she decided, she had to find a way to unleash the ambition within her.

'Caroline, sort your life out', was her mother's favourite tune, especially on days when her horses had let her down. 'You're a black girl, you need to put yourself in order. Don't follow those English girls: their bread already butter.'

Silly mothers. She imagined the same song being sung at the home of each of her friends, tens of mothers in a deafening chorus, like singers with a captive audience of dithering daughters. They were wasting their time, poor fools, couldn't they see that?

For the children's sole aim was to leave Claremont the moment they hit sixteen. Occasionally a boy talked of attending college to study plumbing, decorating or computing, and there was a girl in 5D, Delores Alexander, who promised that one day *she* was going to university to study Economics. But they were exceptions to the future shop assistants, welders, dental technicians and chairmakers who formed the town's invisible workforce.

Like her best friend, Anna Goliath, Caroline couldn't see distance. Her goal was simply to escape after fifth form. To escape school, but with the qualifications for a secretarial job. When one Saturday morning her mother asked her intentions, she replied - the answer coming out of the blue - that she was studying to become a PA to a Managing Director. Typing and filing confidential letters, arranging top-level meetings with finger-snapping efficiency, flying to Ireland on weekly business trips: she had it all figured out, she lied to her mother, she was going to be the linchpin of a small firm. The business faltering, she imagined making cups of milky, sweet tea and cheering everyone up.

That, though, belonged to the future, if it belonged anywhere. Before then she basked in the joy of sport, sang along to pop songs, and practised her dancing in her tiny room without a care in the world. The comforting sun, refreshing sea and cool rivers of the Caribbean were lodged in her memory, the thought of exotic fruits and sweltering days brought a smile to her face on cold winter nights. But, having settled with her parents and two siblings, she knew she had to face reality. The Caribbean was a distant 4000 miles away, and she was here.

Music, dance and sport compensated for the sun and sea reluctantly left behind. They lacked the spontaneity of the games they used to improvise in the sunshine as children, but they were her world now. To outgrow them was to stifle the joy in her young heart.

Unlike Anna, she had quickly accepted winter. There was netball to look forward to, and bracing cross-country runs in the navy-blue skirt that attracted mud like a powerful magnet. And what could compare to a competitive game of hockey on an icy winter's afternoon?

But summer sports were her true love. Designed for athletics, her young body could perform phenomenal feats. Pushing herself to the limit was what she was born to do, she told herself. To run, jump, twist and leap, faster each time and higher, the exhilaration physical and raw, what could rival the thrill of scorching down the track, or defying gravity?

Wearing little beneath her pink cotton dressing-gown, Anna once spent an entire Saturday morning eyeing herself in the mirror. Straining her neck to get a good view of her rear, calves and thighs, she was in love with her body. In the middle of one of their outlandish dances, Anna thrust her chest forward, stiffened her back, and exploded into raptures of self-admiration. Purring, humming, whistling, at fifteen she was a girl with boys on her mind.

Caroline never fully understood this fascination. *Her* body was for skipping, dancing and sprinting, not for examination under a flattering mirror. She didn't get it. When, through tiny eyes, she glimpsed herself in the mirror that Saturday, she saw a long, narrow face, good-looking, with bulging cheeks, beneath a modest Afro, and a wiry body unlikely to grow beyond its current five-three.

The sprints were her main competitive events. And, when she really pushed herself, the four hundred and forty yards, one sapping lap round the grass track to the south of the school. High jump, which she wasn't particularly good at, she performed with enthusiasm, crash-landing in sand the colour of Demerara sugar. Furious at the sand in her hair and clothes, her mother barked and scowled. But who cares about mothers when they are having fun? If sports filled the timetable, she couldn't imagine a happier schoolgirl in England or the Caribbean.

But there was no way of getting away from her academic record. She knew that and sometimes it hurt. Her termly reports could all have been written by the same hand. 'Caroline's lack of effort is sad to see', her tutor had summed up her year in 3Y. 'Her work is one level below her true capabilities, if not two.'

Even then the teachers didn't know the full story. It took Mr Rees's persistent delving to spot the pattern: the deliberate lateness to Religious Education in order to get herself thrown out, the undiagnosed 'allergy' to dissection that excused her from Biology lessons to her daily rendezvous with Anna in the toilet.

Yet, in the few quiet moments of reflection she allowed herself - in bed while her sister watched television, or on her paper round - she recognised that she had ability. She had done well in primary school in SVG, her first report in Claremont had spoken of her potential. What had happened to her in between?

The glib answers of her classmates in English and History might satisfy the teachers but they weren't for her. When was the last time you went to London, she was tempted to ask several times, how many of you have ridden the underground from east to west for the sheer thrill of it? She wanted more from *her* answers. They had to be real, drawn from raw experience. Doing things, not reading about them in dusty old books, that's what it was about for her then.

Still, there were two written pieces she was particularly proud of. An essay about her aunt's wedding had received a 'Very Good' from the Deputy Head, and a short biography of an aunt in

Birmingham, one of the earliest Caribbean immigrants, had been awarded top marks and pinned on the notice board. So there was something there, she knew, there was definitely a flame. But it was low and hesitant. What's going to become of me, she asked herself on the way home that Monday, what am I going to be?

Fortunately, she consoled herself, she wasn't alone in living for the present. Most of the other black girls in 4C had the same dilemma. They attended school, plaited or styled their hair during tutorial, flirted with the boys, compared fashions, practised their dance steps. An essay here, a scrap of homework there, they did the minimum of work to justify their status as pupils.

Taking things as they came, few had any concrete idea of what they wanted or how to go about getting it. There were always jobs in their town - secretarial, in the banks, at the council, manual - there would always be jobs for smart girls prepared to work hard. For those who preferred not to live and work in the same place, London was only an hour away by slow train or free-flowing motorway. Jobs had existed before her arrival in England, Caroline reassured herself, work would always be there for those with commitment.

The route home took Caroline past Telfer School, ancient and proud, with a reputation for scholarship and sport. It even had a theatre, it was rumoured. The school irritated her immensely. Perhaps it was the immaculate blue blazers the juniors wore, or the shiny red blazers of the snooty seniors. Scampering up Blue Hill or running for the bus, the pupils resembled ants in a state of constant excitement.

No wonder Stephanie Young from 4F, a black girl who stood

no nonsense, had drilled one boy in the stomach for staring at her at the bus stop. 'Stupid Telfer bug!' she had pleaded in her defence to the headmaster, 'what was he staring at, why didn't he cast his eyes somewhere else?' Caroline had chuckled at Stephanie's defence, not knowing the impact the school would have on her future.

At that time, the mid-seventies, few Caribbean pupils attended the prestigious Telfer. Five out of a total of five hundred, and perhaps double the number of Asians. Serious-looking pupils, she saw them as snobbish and 'soft'. They whispered rather than talked, wore their shirts in their trousers, too many were ferried there by their parents.

As she was ambling along Highfield Park, thinking of ways to improve her schoolwork, Caroline was taken aback by the sight of a black boy approaching. Swinging his brown leather bag up to shoulder level, he seemed in a world of his own. What caught Caroline's attention wasn't the boy's leisurely pace or the swinging of the bag, but the volume of his singing. From ten metres away she could hear him humming like someone without a care in the world. As he neared her, she could make out the tune clearly.

Maybe she had got it wrong, she told herself. Perhaps *she* was the one the tune was coming from. So easy to make that mistake: to take what's in your mind and place it in someone else's. Such an easy trap to fall into. But no, she quickly realised, it wasn't her, it was definitely him. She shifted her body to the left so that she would be directly in his path. The boy was almost upon her before he caught himself.

'I'm sorry,' he said.

Caroline didn't like his voice. He spoke too carefully for her taste, instead of letting the words tumble out of his mouth.

'And what are you sorry for?' she asked.

'For knocking you over,' he answered.

'You didn't knock me over.'

'For running into you.'

'You didn't run into me.'

'For blocking your path.'

'You didn't block my path.'

'For whatever.'

'For *whatever*?'

'For whatever.'

'You apologise too easily, boy.'

'Do I?'

'Yes.'

'Sorry.'

'You see?'

Caroline stared at him. Five-six, thin, he had soft black hair, neatly combed, greased, and shiny. His dark-brown eyes looked anxious. He was like a deer trapped in the glare of approaching headlights.

'What was that song you were singing?' she continued her interrogation.

'What song?'

'The song you were humming, stupid. The song that was so sweet you forgot to look where you were going.'

'Oh that,' he said, casually, 'it's just a little tune.'

'A little tune? Do you know who you're talking to?'

The song was the hopeless fantasy of a teenage boy. The boy

went silent. He looked startled. His forehead glistened like a shoplifter trapped with the sweets in his pockets.

'It's an old folk song,' he mumbled unconvincingly. 'It's from Cuba. We were learning it this afternoon in Spanish.'

Caroline sang the first verse of the song, taking her time, to show him she knew its exact meaning.

'That's a folk song, is it?' she asked, 'that's the kind of song they teach at your posh school, is it?'

'Stop!' the boy begged, as she repeated the chorus, his embarrassment obvious to her.

'Why? What's the matter?' she asked, relishing his discomfort.

'It's not a folk song.'

'No?'

'No.'

'What is it then?'

'Why bother to ask when you know full well what it is?'

'Do your school friends know the kind of songs you sing?'

'Do I care?' he asked, his voice suggesting he was now gaining in confidence. 'Do I look like friends bother me?'

'Do your parents?'

'What's it to do with them?'

'They might be a bit concerned if they were to find out.'

'Who's going to tell them?'

'*I* might.'

'How will you do that?'

'Simple.'

'How?'

'I'll just knock at the door and reveal everything.'

Theirs was a small town. The tiny Caribbean community

was scattered, with clusters where one least expected. Despite its small size he thought it unlikely that she would know his family: after all, he didn't know hers.

A knowing smile appeared at the corner of his mouth, developing into a huge grin Caroline wanted to remove with a crisp slap.

'Well,' he asked, 'what are you going to do then?'

'I'm not saying. You'll have to wait and see, won't you?'

'You must think I was born yesterday,' he replied with a dismissive chuckle, 'well I wasn't. Even if you knew my parents, what about it? This isn't the West Indies, you know. You can't just waltz up to someone's house and blurt out your nonsense: unless you want to get yourself arrested and carted off to the madhouse. Besides, whatever you tell them I would deny it. I would say *you* were the one singing the song. In fact I'm tempted to broadcast it all over *your* school.'

'Really?'

'Yes, why shouldn't I? You were going to do the same to me, weren't you?'

'It was a joke, you silly boy, I've got better things to do with my time.'

'A joker, are you? Well then, joker, what's your name? And while you're at it, why don't you give us your number?'

There was no way Caroline was going to reveal her real name. Especially to a Telfer school boy with a penchant for adult songs. But there was something about him she admired. One minute he looked timid, the next he was threatening her with the police, and now he was asking her name and number! He had a cheek, he was certainly bold. He was a boy, but he might be fun.

'I don't normally do this,' she said, thinking back to the French class and convinced she had been given a new nickname, 'I don't know why I'm doing it, but my initials are PQ. '

'What does the P stand for?'

'You're supposed to be intelligent, so work it out.'

'Is it Patricia, Pamela?'

'Don't be stupid!'

'Petra? Pauline? Pearl?'

'You're hopeless.'

'Let me try the surname then: there can't be many West Indian names beginning with Q: unless it's something ridiculous like Quintin, or foolish like Quow.'

'You're the most pathetic boy I've ever met. You don't seem to know anything. What's *your* name?'

'Raymond.'

'Raymond What?'

'Pilgrim.'

'Pilgrim? Where did you get that nonsense name?'

'Try my parents.'

'I'd change it if I were you.'

'Well you're not me.'

'Thank goodness for that!'

If only their uniform wasn't so drab, Caroline thought. A grey sock had collapsed into her left shoe, she felt plain in her grey skirt. Her jumper tied around her waist, she wondered what Raymond thought of her. But the conversation ended abruptly, they stood there for an awkward moment, then he went his way, and she, hers.

For the next fortnight she took the bus. On the way home each afternoon she would scramble to the window when it arrived

Feather Your Tingaling

at their meeting place. She expected to see Raymond gambolling along, bag in hand, whistling at the top of his voice, had pictured him waiting patiently for her at the side of the road. But he wasn't. She was happy he wasn't, yet she felt sad. She didn't care for boys, but had he forgotten her already?

July came, end of term, the sports season. As expected, Caroline was selected to represent Claremont at the district sports. She couldn't wait. The athletics competitions were her life. Without them school was simply the place to meet her friends and pass the time before, on Tuesdays and Thursdays, hurrying home to prepare dinner for the family. Mr Rees's encouraging words having long since vanished from her mind, she had reverted to attending Claremont for the sport.

Before school each day, and after, she trained hard, alone, friendships postponed, studying abandoned. On the school track and at her local park she practised her start, powered dozens of times through the middle fifty yards, and worked on her stamina. A winning end to the school year was her goal. She couldn't afford to lose her proud record.

Hot, but with a cooling breeze, ideal conditions for sprinting, the Saturday of the district sports finally arrived. Before a race, in three years of serious competition, Caroline had found a way of conquering her nerves. Confident in her training, and with victories in the school competition behind her, she never allowed herself to be distracted by the other competitors. That Saturday, though, despite her preparations, she was tense. Something wasn't right. Powerfully built, muscle-bound, her rivals resembled nineteen-year olds, not juniors! They looked healthy, confident, they even smelled fit!

One girl in particular unsettled her. Her spikes were attractive and new, and a starting block, a piece of equipment she associated with professionals, intimidating to such a degree that Caroline kept glancing at it as though it had magical powers. As she prepared herself mentally for the last time, going through her routine of focusing on the finishing line, all she could picture was this girl being hurled from the blocks, and everyone else trailing like bow-legged children.

They lined up. Caroline slowed her breathing, drawing in deep breaths and exhaling slow, shallow ones. A long silence. Absolute stillness. She could hear her heart thumping outrageously. Silence. nothing. Then bang! barked the gun.

The sprinters exploded. Caroline coaxed everything from her young body. Wheeling her legs and pumping her arms furiously, she tore down the track. Faster and faster she threw herself, legs straining, breathing so hard she could hear herself like someone awoken by their own snoring. But it was no use: her routine and rhythm disturbed, she was defeated even before the gun. As they dipped for the line she knew she was fourth, well beaten.

She couldn't remember feeling so useless after an event. Her calves raw and painful, she had to hobble to collect her tracksuit and towel, in a sad bundle in her kit-bag at the *Start*. In less than fourteen seconds her world had crumbled, an entire year wasted.

Her first serious defeat. It hurt. Second place wouldn't have satisfied her, but to finish fourth, and by such a wide margin? Caroline felt small, crushed, reduced to nothing. The sprints had been her life, what would take their place?

She needed to be alone. Away from words of consolation, she found a quiet spot on the grass bank where she could pass the time before her other event, the sprint relay. The mile was just finishing as she eased herself onto her towel. She didn't care for distance events, but any race with a sprint finish was worth watching. In the tangle of arms, legs and twisted bodies, spurred on by the screaming, clapping and yelling of teachers, parents, and team mates, Caroline could make out a black boy driving himself towards the line. A few moments later she saw Raymond, hands on knees, struggling for breath, in the middle of a small group of boys heaped on the track.

The relay didn't worry her after that. She ran the final leg, led her team to a respectable third. After the race she went in search of Raymond. She tried the shops and the cafeteria, but she couldn't find him. There was nothing to do but wait for the presentation at five-thirty.

And that's where she saw him again. As they were presenting the medals for the mile she noticed him applauding wildly. She strolled over and dug him firmly in the ribs. He turned to her, his face lit up, then he quickly wiped away the grin.

'What are you clapping like that for, you didn't win, did you?' she said.

'No, I came fourth,' he replied.

'So what are you so happy about then?'

'Happy, who's happy?'

'Well, you are!'

'Am I?'

'You must be, or you wouldn't be cheering like that.'

'It was a good race.'

'You didn't win and you call that a good race! What would have happened if you came first?'

'I don't race to win.'

'You don't race to win? Why do you race then?'

'Because I like running. I used to run to my primary school and back in the West Indies and I've just carried on.'

'You're weird! You must be the strangest West Indian boy in this town!'

'Since you're so good, what did *you* run in and what did *you* come?'

Caroline was tempted to switch events, claim a third in the hundred yards, and fourth in the relay. She didn't. She had lost the individual race, but all of a sudden, losing didn't matter as much as it once did.

'I came fourth in the hundred yards, and our team placed third in the relay.'

'That's not bad: I wish I could do the sprints.'

'Why can't you?'

'I'm no good at short distances.'

'I would never have seen you as a runner, let alone a miler.'

'You can't say that, you don't know me,' Raymond sounded tetchy.

'It's a free country, I can say what I want,' Caroline smiled to show him she hadn't meant it like that.

'Does that apply to me too?' Raymond asked. 'I can say what I want as well?'

'Of course,' she answered, with a lavish sweep of the right hand.

'Then I say I want you to come home with me.'

'I beg your pardon!' Caroline couldn't believe what she had heard.

'A lift,' Raymond couldn't help smiling at the look of horror on her face. 'I can give you a lift home.'

'Oh! You had me worried for a moment,' she said, with a sigh of relief. 'Thanks, but I travelled with some of the girls from my school.'

'They can find their own way home, can't they?'

'Yes, I suppose so.'

'Good,' he explained, 'my mother's picking me up. She should be here soon.'

Those molly-cuddled pupils from Telfer, Caroline was on the verge of saying, can't they make their own way on public transport? But she liked the idea of going home in comfort and style. Of arriving outside her house in Weatherburn Road, slamming the car door noisily to alert her brother and sister to her arrival, and stepping out slowly and elegantly like a famous star.

'You expect me to accept a lift from a stranger?' she asked.

'Nothing *strange* about me.'

'So I'm *strange*, am I?'

'You are. Anyone who is afraid to tell you their name must be weird or have something to hide.'

'My name is Caroline Chatoyer. Happy?'

'It's a beautiful name,' Raymond said.

'I'm sure,' Caroline replied in the same weary voice she had used when Byron Cuffy 'crowned' her 'the prettiest girl at Claremont' before asking for a date.

'Come on, let's go: my mother's waiting.'

Caroline hesitated for an instant. There she was, about to go off with a stranger, a boy she hardly knew. A Telfer boy at that, one fond of lewd songs, and his mother! But, she said to herself with a shrug of the shoulders, why not? For what would life be without its little adventures?

They walked the short journey to the car park in silence. Then Raymond said, in a voice less sure than it had seemed a moment earlier, 'Here we are. Here's our car.'

He opened the back door to the silver Volvo, let her in, then followed.

'Good afternoon, Caroline,' said Raymond's mother, in a strong West Indian accent, reaching over and extending her right hand. 'So nice to meet you.'

'Oh my goodness,' Caroline thought, 'what's that blasted boy been saying? And how do they know my name?'

Caroline held the medium-sized light-blue envelope up to the light of the front room. In the glow of the Saturday morning she studied the writing, neat elegant letters, the words perfectly spaced. A woman's hand, she concluded after careful consideration, or possibly a girl's: no boy she knew took such care with anything that didn't involve cricket, football, dancing, or clothes. Definitely female in style, it was the work of someone determined to create a good impression.

That February she had received her first valentine, an expensive heart-shaped card. But after the surprise and delirium of the red envelope, she had spent weeks agonising over the sender. Anonymity detracted from the enjoyment of the simple message, 'U and me belong 2gether'.

This letter, though, was clearly of a different type. Care had gone into the layout of the address, and effort. With such attention to detail, it seemed a pity to ruin the letter by opening it. The experience was to be savoured, delayed, until anticipation could no longer be restrained. After a forensic examination of the envelope, she tore gently along the fold with her index finger and carefully extracted the letter.

As she read, pleasure slowly mounting in her body, she felt special, warm, the only girl in the town to have received an invitation that Saturday. Then, as the obstacles to accepting the invitation dawned on her, the delight gradually subsided, like a late summer's day fading into a cold evening.

Timing was crucial, Caroline knew from bitter experience, convincing her parents to let her go was seldom easy. Catch her mother in the wrong frame of mind and it was goodbye to sleepovers, window shopping with Anna in Oxford Street, and afternoon discos that stretched from twilight to midnight. You had to pick the right day to strike, the precise moment, and luck had to play its part.

With Mrs Chatoyer, a well-placed bet on the horses counted in your favour. On Saturdays and Sundays, under the influence of a smooth rum, her father could be persuaded to place a deposit on a house on the moon. So, as her mother was dressing for church the following day, Caroline approached, like a messenger delivering an important telegram.

'What is it?' Mrs Chatoyer asked, as she wriggled into a black, knee-length skirt.

'A letter.'

'Today is Sunday, Caroline, the postman doesn't come on Sundays.'

'It came yesterday.'

'So why didn't you give it to me then?'

'I forgot.'

'Well don't just stand there, pass it over.'

'It's not yours, it's for me.'

'For you?' Mrs Chatoyer stopped abruptly. 'Who sending you letters?'

'It's an invitation.'

'What kind of invitation?'

'To a party.'

Mrs Chatoyer resumed the battle with the skirt, tugging roughly at the zip, grimacing as though in severe pain.

'Caroline,' she barked, 'listen, and listen me good.'

'It's nothing like that mom,' Caroline pre-empted her warning about boys, 'it's not what you're thinking.'

'What's it about, then?' her mother asked, in a voice resigned to another letter from the headmaster at Claremont.

Caroline read aloud the letter, modulating her voice to sift out the enthusiasm. She had been invited to a birthday party by her school friend, Claudia, at the end of August, she said. It was more of a picnic than a party, she would be home by nine.

Mrs Chatoyer closed her eyes for an instant, then sighed heavily, as though she had received news that her horse had fallen at the last fence but had managed to drag itself over the finishing line.

'I suppose I should be thankful it's not from some boy,' she said. 'Or another complaint about your work from the school.'

'So I can go?'

Mrs Chatoyer threw her a disapproving look, then surprised

her by announcing straight away, instead of the customary three hours, 'Yes, Caroline you can go. I just hope you're not making a mistake. But I could never stop you from doing what you want, could I?'

'I won't do anything I shouldn't,' Caroline said in her most girlish voice.

'You're damn right you won't,' Mrs Chatoyer, exclaimed, 'not if you want to remain under this roof. Now, see what you've done? You made me swear on a Sunday! Get out of my sight, Caroline, go!'

How many times, Caroline wondered, does a girl lie to her mother before she is eventually found out? White lies, half-truths, evasions, shrugs of the shoulder to plead ignorance, how much does a mother really know about the life her daughter leads?

Winter afternoons bunked to sip sweet sherry at Anna's house while their parents were at work; the change of clothing skilfully hidden in her bag for a trip to London on days of RE and French in the summer; the E59 bus driver who occasionally 'lost his way' on Friday thus delivering her home after six: did it never occur to her mother to demand an explanation? And now, a birthday party for Claudia, a fictitious classmate, no mention of Raymond, no suggestion of a picnic thirty miles from town: lies, evasions, fractions of the truth: was deceit ever worth it?

Caroline was wondering this as she strolled with Raymond after their picnic lunch. The afternoon sun on their backs, it was a perfect day for outdoors. Intruders in a landscape of wild cooing birds, fluttering butterflies, and insects on journeys with destinations known only to themselves, they stooped to observe, careful not to disturb the life before them. The noisy vehicles and bustle of town were a world away. They had been walking for forty minutes, chasing pheasants, pausing to identify the sounds of the wildlife, when Raymond stopped at the corner of a field, and Caroline followed. He beckoned to her and they sat on a wooden bench roughly nailed together.

'I'm glad you came,' Raymond began, snapping a dry twig in half.

'So am I,' Caroline replied, 'I'm having a wonderful time.'

'We come here every year in the summer.'

'We go camping in Oxfordshire in July or early August, depending on the weather. The site we go to has lots of red kites. It's magical just watching them hang in the air, no effort at all.'

'You like birds?'

'Don't you? Don't you think they're graceful and elegant?'

'They are, but I couldn't tell the difference between a robin and a hawk. Do you know about trees as well?'

'Deciduous trees shed their leaves, evergreen trees don't: that's all they taught us in science.'

'You can come back with us next year,' Raymond suggested. 'I'll name them for you.'

'A year is a long time.'

'Not really: before you blink spring will be here.'

'Do you always plan that far ahead?' Caroline asked, for she preferred to live from day to day.

'Don't you?'

'No, I just take things as they come.'

'I can't. I'll never get my school work done,' Raymond explained.

'How many subjects are you taking?'

'Eleven, plus Latin.'

'Twelve subjects!' Caroline gasped. 'My goodness! I'm only doing seven: if you include French, which I'm going to fail.'

'How can you be so sure?' Raymond asked, cleaning his hand from the twig.

'I'm rotten at it.'

'I can help you, my French isn't bad.'

'No thanks, I'll just concentrate on the other six.'

'You don't want my help, you mean?'

'I didn't say that. I'm just being pragmatic. With so many subjects, how and when are you going to find the time?'

'I will always find time for you,' Raymond said, aching to take her hand to show her he was sincere.

'*Will* you now?' Caroline asked, in a playful sing-song voice.

'You know that.'

'I don't know anything,' Caroline said, equally playfully, and turning to him. 'And I certainly don't know anything about *you*.'

'Do you want to?'

Raymond fidgeted with his hands in his pockets. But neither would leave their sanctuary to take Caroline's hand.

'I'm not sure,' Caroline snorted. 'Any boy who sings the kind of songs you sing at the top of their voice on their way home from school sounds like trouble to me.'

'And you don't like trouble?'

'Which girl does?'

'Some do,' Raymond said, adding swiftly, 'So I've heard.'

'Well this one doesn't,' Caroline said firmly.

'That's fine by me,' said Raymond with a shrug of the shoulders.

'Raymond, is that why you invited me along?' Caroline asked, looking him directly in the eye. 'Because you thought I might be a *certain* kind of girl?'

'Think about it,' Raymond answered. 'Would I have sent you an invitation if I thought you were like that?'

'I suppose not,' she said.

'No, it's because I like you.' Raymond could feel the words pouring out. 'You're clever, you're argumentative, you always come up with a surprising answer.'

'Do I?'

'Yes, you do. That's why I enjoy your company so much.'

'But we don't have anything in common,' Caroline pointed out. 'You go to your posh school where everyone does *fifty* subjects, and I attend Claremont where you're lucky to scrape six.'

'We have more in common than you think,' Raymond tried to reassure her.

'Such as?'

'We both grew up in the Caribbean, we like music and sports, and we enjoy school.'

'Where did you get that idea?' Caroline cackled at the suggestion that school was something to be enjoyed.

'I just assumed.'

'Well you're wrong. I like school, but not in the way *you* obviously do. And I certainly don't *enjoy* it.'

Surprised by this revelation, Raymond asked, 'The teachers?'

'They do their job,' Caroline replied, 'I can't fault them for trying. But they're out five seconds after the finishing bell, just like the pupils. Harold Nedd went to Barbados for three months and they hardly noticed. When he came back Mrs Ramsaywhack asked if he had got over the flu, he said yes, and that was the end of the matter!'

'The pupils?'

'Some like school, but for most it's a place to go to until they shove you out to get a job. Like La Neige Daniels says, the only reason she goes is to meet her friends and pass the time. Instead of having to loiter in the town centre, it's a warm place where people leave her alone.'

'What about you?'

'I don't wake up screaming in the night, but I wouldn't say it's my favourite place.'

'There must be bits you enjoy.'

'Games, friends, dinners, and I do like *some* subjects - Physics, English and Maths: although the topic we're doing at the moment, binary numbers, is way above my head. Where in the world would anyone use them?'

'They're fun, they're quirky: I love them.'

Caroline threw Raymond a funny look, as though he had gone mad. 'Poor you,' she said.

'Lucky me, you mean.'

'You must have a better teacher than me, then, if you find them fascinating.'

'Why don't you put in for a transfer?' Raymond suggested.

'Where to?'

'Telfer.'

'Telfer?'

'Why not? If you pass your seven subjects you're guaranteed a place.'

'Do you think I'm good enough for Telfer?'

'Of course you are.'

'Answer me honestly Raymond, do you think I could make it there?'

'You're just as clever as most of the girls in my year, believe me.'

'You're not just saying that, are you?'

'I wouldn't lie about something like that.'

'So I would survive at Telfer?'

'You wouldn't just survive, you would prosper.'

'But it would mean leaving all my friends behind!'

'You could see them at the weekend, the town isn't *that* big.'

'It won't be the same.'

After the initial excitement, a wave of sadness engulfed Caroline. Doubts began to gather. 'And, just in case you haven't noticed,' she said, 'it's mostly white girls at Telfer.'

'So what, are you afraid of white people?'

'Of course not,' she replied quickly, 'but I wouldn't feel comfortable. I'll be tense all day. I'll feel they're just waiting for me to mess up so they could laugh out loud. Heaven knows what they'll be saying behind my back!'

'The boys aren't like that,' Raymond explained. 'I'm black, I'm from the Caribbean, I have an accent, but they accept me for who I am. And I'm positive the girls are the same. Inevitably you get the odd idiot, but I'm sure it's the same at Claremont.'

'I wish I could believe that.'

'There's only one way to find out. Put in your application and make sure you get your subjects.'

'I'll think about it,' Caroline promised.

For the next forty minutes they talked like this, Raymond trying to dispel her fears, Caroline warming to the prospect of sixth form study yet fearful of being separated from the friends who had smoothed her path into an English secondary school.

To ascend to a world of privilege, high expectations, and whispered prejudices, did she really want that? What would her friends say? How would they see her? As a traitor, an upstart, or would they wish her well?

As Raymond coaxed she agreed one moment, resisted stoutly the next. For a girl from her background there was much to gain but more to lose. Each time the conviction of its rightness took hold, her poor grades reignited the doubts. Every word of encouragement brought to her mind the picture of Telfer, its tree-lined perimeter a warning to keep out unless you met its stringent entry criteria of wealth and academic ability.

She recalled her first day at Claremont, a freezing Tuesday, the weight of the unfamiliar coat on her back, Anna taking her trembling hand and leading her into the classroom. The sea of unfamiliar faces, black, white, Asian, pupils with their feet on the desks, teachers struggling to keep order, 'Help!' she had wanted to scream. She was happy there now, did she really want the aggravation of starting anew?

An hour later, the sun dull but persistent, a slight wind tempering its lazy heat, Raymond and Caroline dragged themselves from the bench and set off to rejoin the others. Their first proper conversation. They were no longer the singing boy on Blue Hill and the crushed athlete at the district sports. Their hopes shared, and their fears, they were bound by wanting the best for each other. On the way they identified clouds and planes with wispy trails high in the sky, holding hands as though they couldn't bear to be separated. As they neared their destination, with Raymond's suggestion still fresh in her mind, Caroline reflected on the day.

The anxiety of meeting his parents had dissipated the instant she entered their home. A middle-aged Caribbean couple, Mr Pilgrim intent on doing as little as possible on a warm day, his wife fussy, tidying and cleaning as though for an imminent visit by the Queen, Caroline felt comfortable in their company. There was no need to try to make an impression.

Mrs Pilgrim was short, heavily-built and round-shouldered, her husband thin and erect but not much taller, with a face that suggested he had never known a sad day. With glasses and grey hair, he could have been her uncle Lawrence, a fisherman, in Dominica. Warm and unassuming, they included her in their plans, treated her as a daughter. She had had to help load the car and to pitch the tent, had giggled when, at lunch, Mrs Pilgrim finished her husband's stout and when, a few minutes later, in retaliation, her husband hid her pipe primed with strands of pungent black tobacco. Playful, constantly sparring, they reminded her of her own parents.

But Raymond was the reason she was there. Its belt loosely buckled, his stone trousers fitted him perfectly. A baggy, orange T shirt complemented the lively blackness of his skin. His hair, worn short against the current trend, clung tight to his head, accentuating the narrow face, handsome but with a wisp of sadness. In Raymond Pilgrim, bouncing along with the gaiety of their first encounter, hardworking, ambitious for her, she had found a boy she could be friends with. And more.

Four of them had driven the thirty miles to the picnic in the family Volvo. Had spent two tiring hours erecting the tent, rested, eaten, then paired off to explore the countryside. Now, hungry and thirsty again, Caroline and Raymond arrived back at the site just after four.

A born worrier, fastidious, Mrs Pilgrim had ordered her husband to check the front door before setting off to the picnic. At Tring where he had briefly exceeded the speed limit, Caroline had observed the severe black woman's look she gave him. With a weak, apologetic smile, as they began their walk, she had directed that the first to return check the safety of the car. So now, following her instructions, Raymond strolled to the car park, leaving Caroline to go to the tent.

As she entered, Caroline recoiled as though a cobra has positioned itself to spit at her. She recoiled, she froze. Her body was paralysed as her brain laboured to interpret the image her eyes had transmitted. For there, squatting on the blanket was Mr Rees, gorging himself on the potato salad she had prepared for the picnic.

To meet a teacher away from school, at a petrol station or in the shops was an exceptional event, once a year, if that frequent. Teachers belonged to a different world, socially and geographically. In four years of secondary school she had glimpsed one in the local supermarket, and sat momentarily with her back to another in the public library while researching a History project. Socially, therefore, the sight of a teacher was as likely as a flurry of snow in high June. How then to explain the presence of the French master on a family outing? It had to be an illusion, she told herself, a cruel trick of the darkness of the tent.

'Caroline,' Mr Rees blurted out through a mouthful, after

what seemed an eternity, 'what are you doing here?'

Caroline imagined that, his tent pitched nearby, he had stumbled into theirs by mistake and, like Goldilocks, finding no one in, had decided to help himself. She tried to speak but her mouth refused its instructions from the brain. It simply couldn't be him! Admittedly, the man knew her name, and was complimenting her on her potato salad by devouring huge portions, but surely not! It couldn't be, could it?

In a cream cotton shirt, turquoise sports jacket, black jeans and brown sandals, Mr Rees still resembled a teacher. His clothes detracted not one iota from his school manner. He continued to chomp until, from the expression on her face, he realised her predicament. So he motioned for her to enter and invited her to sit next to him.

'Mr Rees, what are you doing here?' Caroline eventually stammered, when it was clear that it wasn't a ghost or an intruder.

'I'm a friend of the Pilgrims.'

'You are?' Caroline asked, thinking to herself, 'But you're English, you can't be!'

'Yes, I've known them for several years.'

'I don't understand,' Caroline admitted, for it wasn't obvious how their social spheres intersected.

'I'm Raymond's private tutor,' Mr Rees explained, with the reluctance of someone betraying a secret.

Caroline had fetched herself a drink, passion fruit juice, ice cold and bitter-sweet. The glass shook in her hand as though she had been struck a blow flush on the elbow.

'Raymond has private lessons?' she asked, bewildered, bemused. 'Raymond Pilgrim?'

'For Latin, yes.'

'I didn't know that.'

'Didn't he tell you?'

'No,' she confessed sadly, 'we've only been friends for a little while.'

'Where did you two meet?'

'At the district sports in July. Raymond's quite a good miler.'

'I know. He loves his sports. And he has the same problem you do when it comes to Latin: he doesn't learn the vocabulary, he doesn't practise his grammar. But then he's more of a scientist than a linguist. Even so I expect him to get an *A*. And with a bit more effort I'm sure *you* are capable of getting a *B* for your French, and the same for Maths, English, Geography and History.'

'Who me?' Caroline was surprised at this assessment of her abilities.

'That's what your teachers say.'

'Do they?'

'Yes.'

'Honestly?'

'Honestly,' Mr Rees repeated. 'They all agree on the same thing: if you dedicate yourself to your studies you could do quite well. You have a sound basic knowledge and your writing's quite good when you put your mind to it. All you lack is application.'

At this point Raymond returned. After they had exchanged greetings, Raymond poured himself a glass of mauby and squatted on the blanket on Mr Rees's right flank.

'Caroline told me you two met at the district sports,' Mr Rees said to Raymond, finishing his potato salad and starting on a small bowl of rice positioned on the ground in front of him.

'Yes we did,' Raymond answered, thankful that she hadn't mentioned their first encounter, although he knew, instinctively, that she wouldn't share their secrets with anyone.

'Caroline's one of our stars at Claremont,' Mr Rees explained to Raymond, 'she's our sprint champion.'

'I know, I saw her run the hundred yards.'

'I hope you don't mind, Raymond,' Mr Rees continued, but I told her about your Latin.'

'That's not a problem,' Raymond shrugged his shoulders to show he wasn't bothered. 'Everyone needs help with something.'

'I also told her she needs to work harder on *her* lessons, especially her French.'

'I offered to help but she turned me down,' Raymond explained.

'I didn't turn you down,' Caroline interjected, surprised at the easy relationship between teacher and pupil, 'I said you would be too busy with your own work. With a dozen subjects time must be quite tight.'

'Raymond's extremely well organised, Caroline,' said Mr Rees, answering for Raymond, 'you should at least consider his offer. You need to get those grades up.'

'Caroline's thinking of joining the sixth from at Telfer,' said Raymond, looking across to Caroline as he did so, as though everything had been settled. 'Aren't you?'

'Excellent idea,' said Mr Rees through a mouthful of rice, before Caroline could respond. 'Now that's what I call good news. That's just the motivation you need.'

'I'd like to but I'm not sure,' Caroline admitted. 'GCEs are hard enough, heaven knows what sixth form work must be like. I don't know if I could handle the pressure. And even if I did get a transfer, what would I study?'

'Which would you say are your best subjects?' Mr Rees asked.

'History, English and Physics, I suppose.'

'That's an unusual combination.'

'They're the subjects I enjoy the most.'

'The Physics looks a bit peculiar.'

'I like the practical bits. We did some experiments on circuits which really made me think.'

'And the theory, would you say you've got a strong grasp?'

'Of the basics, yes. But some of the ideas are way above my head.'

'Then you'll struggle at A level. How's your Maths? '

'I like probability, geometry and Algebra. But if there's binary numbers at A level then, no thanks.'

'Mr Billingy says you've got a logical brain, so Maths is probably a better bet.'

'Possibly. But I still don't know if I would like it at Telfer.'

'Why not?'

'I'm not sure I'll fit in.'

'In what way?' asked Mr Rees.

'Well, 'I'll be leaving my friends behind, won't I?'

'Your friends would understand,' Mr Rees insisted. 'If they're true friends they would want the best for you. And if you're thinking what I think you are, there are plenty of girls of similar ability at Telfer.'

'But not black girls.'

'No, maybe not. But you'll find the girls are not that

dissimilar: they are teenage girls with teenage concerns. In any case, if you're really worried, why not get some of the other Caribbean pupils to apply for a transfer too? All they need is to work hard to get the grades.'

Caroline worked. Through autumn and winter, during the mild spring and summer that never outgrew its wetness. Shut away in her tiny room, as she had for her sprinting, she developed a routine and stuck to it: two hours of study each day after school, Saturdays off, and three hours of revision on Sunday evenings after a spot of television. Her textbooks neatly laid out on the dressing table, with four years to catch up, friendships couldn't interfere with her pattern. Studying became her sport.

No single method satisfied her, she was a girl who believed in variety. Going by what seemed natural at the time, she trusted her instincts. Whatever suggested itself, she followed. Reading aloud, she listened acutely to her essays, and judged them by their sound. Where they lacked rhythm, or just didn't sound right, she struck out the passage and began again. In this way she learned to write with confidence. By November she could write a solid essay within three days.

A new world, one of facts, argument, theories and ways of reasoning opened up before her. Geography, History or Maths, or any of the other four, once she tore into a subject she couldn't let go. On a bench in Highfield Park after school, at the swings or in the library, Anna tested her French vocabulary, shuffling the cards of words and phrases they had made themselves, until they both knew every suit by heart. To address her shaky graph work, Caroline carefully drew each curve in her notebook, scribbling its properties below, and reciting them until they stuck. Each curve became a little person with its own personality, every equation solved drove her to another, more daunting and complex, or to a fresh topic in algebra or geometry.

She studied. She visualised sitting the exams, imagined herself opening the papers and, finding her favourite topics, coasting through them as in a race against junior sprinters.

The whole year was like this, everything in its place. School, study, her Saturday job in a supermarket, a Sunday run in the park. There was the occasional trip to London to ride the underground with Raymond and Anna, they went to the cinema, or attended the odd Friday disco at Newlands Club. She went walking with Raymond in Highfield Park, they played, held hands, kissed. In her cramped bedroom and in the comfort of hers, they revised, silently, or sometimes together. Puzzled by her absence from their games and fooling around, stuck in their ways, her friends looked on, then returned to their hair worship, learning the latest dances, and flirting with boys. Her life wasn't for them, just as theirs wasn't for her.

In June the exams came, a wet and windy fortnight in a summer for cardigans. Caroline wrote till her fingers were tired, the words gushed from her pen with a fluency that amazed and gratified her. As she left the examination room for the last time, her fate in the lap of the examiners, she was relieved it was over. Yet, as she walked slowly home, a feeling of emptiness overcame her, her stomach felt tight. Memories of the afternoon at the district sports came flooding back. She hoped it wasn't an omen.

Too anxious to catch the bus, terrified of what the envelope might contain, she ran all the way home from Claremont with the results on that fateful August Thursday. Alone, in the quiet of the house, she lowered herself onto the bed, closed her eyes and whispered a prayer. This was it.

Bracing herself, she opened the envelope and lingered over the results. A smile grew on her lips, the slight curl widening until she was brimming. Gently, ever so gently, she punched the air with a firm fist. She had done it. Later that evening, her mother crying with joy, her father beaming with pride, toasting her success with a small rum, Caroline collapsed onto the settee and slept for a solid hour. Had Raymond not come round for a joint celebration, she might have slept through the night.

That was just the beginning. A place at Telfer confirmed, she became aware of a new feeling within her. It was a feeling of terror, panic. Faint to begin with, it grew every day until she began to dread meeting her friends and having to explain her decision, her success, her 'desertion'. She wasn't good enough for Telfer, she kept telling herself, she had only got in by cramming, she would never truly make the grade. For weren't all their students doing twelve subjects? Wouldn't her miserable two *A*s, four *B*s and a *C* leave her cruelly exposed?

In late August, on a day when these feelings momentarily subsided, she accompanied her mother to buy her new uniform, textbooks, new shoes, and PE kit. Although the red blazer was a cool fit, and she couldn't wait to show off to Raymond, as she paraded for her mother she felt a fraud. Don't waste your money, she felt like saying to Mrs Chatoyer, as they headed for the counter, I've changed my mind. I've decided to stay on in the sixth form at Claremont. That secretarial job I told you about will do me fine.

She tried to be brave. As she watched her mother counting

the money she had saved assiduously, she told herself she would be fine. Pull yourself together, girl, she kept saying in her mind, what are you afraid of, the pupils, the teachers, the work?

She could never find the answer. Individually, teachers, pupils, work didn't daunt her. But somehow, thrown into their world, an intruder into a settled community, one where the pupils were reputedly rich and clever, wasn't she bound to come off worse?

The time flew by. Autumn continued the rainy summer. Before she knew it, the Sunday before her move to Telfer had arrived. For a year she had thought of little else and now it was here. That night she felt sick. Her stomach ached, she couldn't sleep. Tossing and turning, bathed in warm sweat, why was the feeling that Telfer was going to be a disaster so powerful?

On a cold Friday near the end of her first term, as she was packing away her books, Mrs Wilson, her form tutor and maths teacher, beckoned for Caroline to stay behind after the lesson. It was time for a 'little chat'. Mrs Wilson was a slight woman in her fifties. Caroline sometimes saw her on the way to school, pedalling furiously on a bicycle that could have succeeded the Penny Farthing. Not knowing what to expect that dull evening, the light in the classroom unnaturally bright, her mind began to search desperately for a reason. Did someone complain about her? Had she ventured into some forbidden region of the school? Had she broken some ancient rule?

The chair felt uncomfortable beneath her. Her heart galloped, her skin felt and smelled sour with sweat.

'How is it going, Caroline?' Mrs Wilson began.

'Fine,' Caroline replied, in an uncertain voice, forcing a smile and packing her books with exaggerated care.

'Yours lessons?'

'Fine.'

'Up to date with your homework?'

'Yes.'

Mrs Wilson came and sat beside her. She smelled of flowers, and the layers of foundation on her thin face gave the impression of a woman who didn't believe in mirrors.

'How have you settled in?' she asked.

'Okay,' Caroline tried to sound chirpy, for she wasn't sure of the drift of Mrs Wilson's conversation.

'Couldn't have been easy.'

Caroline relaxed a bit. She didn't know the reason for the 'little chat', but the tone of the teacher's voice gave her the confidence to be frank, as did her closeness.

'No,' she admitted, 'the first month was very difficult.'

'In what way?' Mrs Wilson encouraged her to elaborate with a sweep of the right hand.

'Well, all the students were friends, and if not friends, at least they knew each other. I was an outsider. No one had time for me. Everyone already had their little group, no one seemed to want an extra friend.'

'Was it that bad?'

'Yes, it was. There were days when I wanted to run away and never come back.'

'How did you cope?'

'I just put my head down and got on with it. I was always in the library, I was first into the woods during cross country, I worked hard to get into the hockey team.'

'How are things now?'

'Better. It's as though the buildings have shrunk to my size. Before, they were so huge I felt small, lost. Just finding the classrooms was a challenge. I got fed up asking directions.'

'Go on.'

'Everyone was helpful but no one actually asked why I didn't know my way around. It was as if they weren't seeing me. What was the point of being here if everyone is too busy to notice me? That's what I kept asking myself.'

'You wanted to be noticed?'

'Yes. Funnily enough, yes: I wanted to be noticed, but I didn't want anyone to notice me. I didn't want special treatment.'

'I'm not sure I understand,' Mrs Wilson admitted. 'And now?'

'There's a small group I go round with. There's me and Sharon Dalrymple and Edna Thomas. We're all taking the same subjects. Sharon's a sports fanatic and Edna's into drama. It's like Mr Rees said, the girls aren't that different.'

'Godfrey said that, did he?' Mrs Wilson asked.

'Who's Godfrey?'

'Godfrey Rees.'

'Do you know him?'

'Yes. We occasionally meet at curriculum events.'

'What a small world!' Caroline exclaimed.

'Indeed it is,' said Mrs Wilson. 'Indeed it is. Now, the reason I asked you to stay behind is this.'

Mrs Wilson got up and ambled to her desk. Caroline watched her pick up a sheet of paper and begin the journey back to where she was sitting in the middle of the classroom. Her heart began to thump. With her easy manner, her pretence at listening and caring, Mrs Wilson had set a trap and what had *she* done? She had fallen right in, hadn't she? For, surely the paper she was holding had to be about her! Acting concerned, smiling and nodding sympathetically, she was now preparing to drop some bad news: wasn't that how some teachers operated?

Caroline steeled herself. Whatever Mrs Wilson had to throw at her, she would hurl back. She would give as good as she got. She belonged at Telfer, her hard work had got her there. Raymond and Mr Rees had encouraged her, Anna had helped in her revision, but no one at Telfer had done her favours. The hard slog had been hers and hers only. She wasn't top of the class but she was holding her own. At first she had been intimidated by the historic buildings, the stern faces of past benefactors, and the diligence of the pupils, but no one could doubt her right to be there!

'I want to make sure you're well prepared for the Christmas exams,' Mrs Wilson said, carefully perusing the paper. 'Your Maths is fine, I know, but I just want to check your English and History. These tests are important and since you're new to the school, I'm just checking that you appreciate that: we mustn't leave anything to chance, must we?'

Caroline let out a sigh of relief. Fancy putting herself through all that, she thought! Fancy letting her imagination run away with her like that! She sighed again. It was so easy to let fears and doubts cloud her judgement.

'I've been getting *B*s in my homework,' she replied proudly, 'and I've already started on the revision packs.'

'So you're confident of getting a good pass in all your subjects?'

'Yes.'

'Good,' Mrs Wilson laid a warm hand on her shoulder. 'But don't forget, if you need my help, don't be afraid to ask. The teachers here are quite approachable - mostly. Mustn't leave anything to chance, must we?'

Two years later, the envelope with the exam results resting proudly on the coffee table, her mother beaming with pride, a tear rolling down her father's cheek, Mrs Wilson's words came back to her. 'Mustn't leave anything to chance, must we?'

What part does chance play in our lives? Caroline wondered. Does chance work for everyone, or does it pick and choose? It had thrown her Raymond, then Mr Rees, and finally, Mrs Wilson. How did chance work?

She didn't know the answer. Chance chose, that's what mattered. She had seized the chance, acted on impulse when, on another day, she would have given Raymond a dismissive glance and continued her journey. The singing boy, the surprising miler, the boy who liked her foolish questions, the first boy to be candid with her, the boy who had held her hand so tight she knew they would never be separated, chance had delivered him to her. He had infected her just as much as she had infected him. He knew when to be around, he knew when she wanted to be left alone staring out the window or at the sky. He knew when she needed kissing, he could tell when holding hands was just the thing.

As she waited for Raymond's visit to her house to celebrate their A level success together, her mother selecting her horses with the concentration that cost her equally in sanity and money, her father sipping a small brandy, she joined her father and raised a glass to chance and impulse.